HEART OF PROPHECY

CONNOR WHITELEY

No part of this book may be reproduced in any form or by any electronic or mechanical means. Including information storage, and retrieval systems, without written permission from the author except for the use of brief quotations in a book review.

This book is NOT legal, professional, medical, financial or any type of official advice.

Any questions about the book, rights licensing, or to contact the author, please email connorwhiteley@connorwhiteley.net

Copyright © 2021 CONNOR WHITELEY

All rights reserved.

DEDICATION

Thank you to all my readers without you I couldn't do what I love.

CHAPTER 1

The snake always hides in the flowers.

Alessandria knew that fact like the back of her hands. Especially, as her father had drummed it into her over the years before his unfortunate death.

She kept looking straight ahead at a rather stunning painting of a naval battle from over a few hundred years ago. Alessandria wasn't exactly sure what her favourite piece of the picture was. The immense brushstrokes that highlighted the violent waves crashing against the two immense fleets. The little details of the soldiers on the harbour preparing for the ground assault. She was impressed she could make out the faces of the soldiers. Or the little flicks of the paintbrush on the ships that showed the massive flames that worked their way through the fleets.

Alessandria had to smile at this painting and she understood why her father loved it. But it was a little big to have in the castle. So keeping it at the Art Gallery would have to do for now.

The sound of people murmuring and chatting quietly reminded her she wasn't alone. Alessandria didn't have to turn to know there were tens or even hundreds of sweaty people around her. Here to admire Ordericous' finest art.

But Alessandria would have preferred to bring some essential oils with her. It was a recent trick the nobility had discovered that if you wipe a little bit of the oil under your nose. Then you don't need to smell the sweaty common folk.

Granted Alessandria despised the rest of the nobility for discriminating against the commoners, but she could understand it now as a massive whiff of foul body odour washed over her.

She almost gagged.

Also, Alessandria realised she had to keep her mouth very still. Otherwise, her mouth tasted foul salt and other horrid tastes.

Turning her attention back to the immense painting, Alessandria wondered how the criminals wanted to get this out. It was massive after all. They certainly couldn't carry it out.

She raised an eyebrow.

What if they were going to steal it at night?

The thought had crossed her mind earlier but Alessandria knew her merchant friend was never wrong. He said the painting was being taken today before closing time. And Alessandria believed him.

Then she remembered the bottle of fine wine the merchant had given her as payment for... not investigating him.

She hardly mind not investigating the merchant. After all he told her everything she needed to protect the people on her land so he wasn't a problem. Yet Alessandria would arrest him if he ever hid a threat from her.

The feeling of warmth washed over her neck as she was reminded of that silly little row of windows that went across the top of the Gallery.

She brushed some of her long hair over her neck. Wanting to find this criminal and get out of here.

The sound of a massive wooden stick hitting the polished black marble floor made Alessandria smile as Hellen came to stand next to her.

Alessandria gave Hellen a quick look and almost laughed at her friend's black leather boots covered in mud and her equally muddy grey Procurator cloak.

"You do know someone's going to have to clear that up," Alessandria said.

"Ya but I gonna job to do,"

Alessandria had to agree with her there. Hellen was a dedicated Procurator, a lot more than others.

"Why ya looking at some old painting? We should be hunting that crook,"

"Patience," Alessandria said.

Turning her head slightly, Alessandria looked at the crowd to see the crowd of tourists part a little, almost like someone was coming through.

"I see that crook," Hellen said, walking into the crowd.

Turning around fully, Alessandria saw all the crowds of people in their full sweaty mass. There were people everywhere all chatting and pointing to the breath-taking works of art.

As she walked into the crowd, sliding past different people and smelling their sweat and the oil from their work, Alessandria carefully walked towards the target.

She saw the crowd move a little as someone slowly walked towards her.

Placing a hand on one of her long swords, she gave a small smile as its cold metal hilt felt good in her hand.

A moment later, the crowd opened a final time to reveal an extremely short little man, maybe a metre tall, wearing posh expensive silk. But his face was rough and worn. Probably after decades of hard labour.

He walked up to Alessandria, thinking he would pass her, Alessandria stood her ground.

The man looked up.

Alessandria grinned at him.

His eye's widened.

He snapped out a gun.

He fired.

Alessandria jumped out the way.

Landing elegantly on the ground. Before jumping back up.

People screamed.

They ran.

The little man was lost in the crowd.

Alessandria surged forward.

Pushing people away.

She had to find her target.

Alessandria saw the crowd opening.
She saw the criminal.
Another gunshot went off.
Was Hellen in trouble?
The thought made Alessandria's heart race.
She charged forward.
Knocking people to the ground.
The smell of sweat was immense.
The crowd opened up as she ran.
Another shot went off.
Someone cried and screamed.

Knocking a final person to the ground. Alessandria charged into the opening.

Only to see Hellen whacking the little man with her massive stick.

The man went flying.

Smashing his head into a priceless painting. His blood spraying up the canvas.

Walking over to the little man, Alessandria looked at him shaking her head. All this silly criminal wanted was a painting that wasn't his. This was theft plain and simple. She so badly wanted to arrest him, but as this wasn't Fireheart Land she couldn't.

Hellen came over. Whacking her stick into the back of his head.

With one almighty crack, the man fell unconscious.

"Thank ya, Alexis," Hellen said. "That should keep my Dominicus Procurator off my back for a while,"

Looking at the pool of blood under the man's head, Alessandria wasn't that sure if Hellen's boss would be too pleased.

A tall poshly dressed woman, probably the Head of The Gallery, walked around the corner of the art Gallery, looked at the blood and screamed in horror. Not at the body but at the painting.

She rushed over.

She looked at Alessandria.

Alessandria pointed at Hellen.

The Head of the Gallery looked at Hellen.

"I think it adds character to ya painting," Hellen said.

The Head of the Gallery turned around and quickly walked away.

A part of Alessandria wanted to think about how this Head would explain the damage worth tens of thousands of coins to the owner. But that was not her problem for now, at least.

Alessandria's eyes widened as she saw a tall stunning man walk around the corner of the Gallery in his typically well-fitting black and fiery red armour. Highlighting his muscles and face perfectly. It was Nemesio.

She wanted to wonder how the former Inquisitor who almost cost her family everything was still working with her. But after their date a month ago, she wanted to keep him around.

"Lady Fireheart," Nemesio said.

"That is oddly formal of you Nemesio. What's

up?" Alessandria said.

"Your mother has returned, and she *needs* to see you. She knows about the Seeker,"

CHAPTER 2

I really hate waiting. I absolutely hate it with a passion. When someone sets a meeting and I arrive on time, not early, I expect the other person to be ready.

After all, I am Daniel Fireheart, I am how the military gets its weapons and soldiers. And I can't believe I'm saying this but I would like to become 'friends' with this Head of The Military after we killed the last one.

Shaking my head, I frowned at literally everything. Everything in this little corridor was awful. From the disgusting and utterly dull grey rough rock that lined the walls and the curved ceiling to the dull grey floor. It wasn't even polished.

Now I think about it judging by the smell of this corridor that smelt like damp mould. That left a strange foul taste in my mouth. I think this is a bit of a strange place for the Head of the Military to have their office.

At the thought of being sent to the wrong place on purpose, I span my dull blade with my hand and took deep breaths to calm myself.

The sound of little claws tapping the ground made me roll my eyes at the thought of rats. I really didn't need rats. Not that I don't like them but I can't be bothered to kill anything today.

Looking around and ignoring my hate for this corridor, I tried to remember what Alessandria wanted me to ask him. Oh yes, don't punch him and tried to get us better pay.

Both those comments made me smile a little. Just because I'm autistic and hate certain people with a passion doesn't mean I'm going to punch him. But I suppose she could be referring to the so-called incident the other week when a servant was annoying me so I broke his nose.

Then the other comment I was a bit puzzled by because of how well the Queen and the Military pays us anyway. And it's not like our noble family needs any money.

The sound of high heels tapping against the solid rock made me turn and give a false smile to see a tall elegant woman in 9-inch black heels and a supposedly stunning dress that clung to her figure walked towards me.

She wandered up to me and stopped to one side. Then the thunderous sound of footsteps stomped down the hall after her.

My dull blade spun quicker.

Looking up the corridor to see who it was, I rolled my eyes as an immensely overweight man dressed in horrific leather clothes stomped towards me.

I don't know what I was more surprised about. The ugly leather clothes or the fact his breakfast practically covered it. Judging by the food he probably had eggs and some creamy sauce.

Clearly nothing like my nobility breakfast of salmon on some weird posh bread served on a bed of whale eggs. But of course, he didn't need to know that.

Again I rolled my eyes at myself as I was surprised I was being this judge-y towards someone of a lower class. I think it was clear I didn't like him.

"You must be the Freak Daniel Fireheart. The weird boy with a taste for men," he said.

My eyebrows rose at the judgement in his voice.

"I am Daniel Fireheart. I am not a Freak,"

"Of course not. I'm sure it is perfectly normal for boys to like boys. I think the Inquisition should have dealt with you correctly,"

Flashes of the Inquisition stabbing, slashing and burning me flooded my mind.

My arms felt like they were on fire.

My ancient self-inflicted cuts burned as did the newer ones from the Inquisition.

The dull blade in my hand spun as fast as it could.

I was more than happy to kill this mortal fool.

"I can show you how the Inquisition treats people," I said.

"I'm sure you would love that Freak but I am unavailable,"

Now I really wanted to kill him. Yet I needed

to at least try to keep my promise to Alessandria.

"I came here wanting to be friends, Head of the Military. That will not be happening. I also came here to inform you the House of Fireheart are doubling our prices," I said.

The man's eyes narrowed. Sweat dripped off his forehead.

"I... will not pay those prices,"

His disgusting odour of fear and his breakfast whiffed into my nose. I gagged.

"You do not have a choice. The House of Fireheart controls the Weapon Industry. One word from me and everything from the blacksmiths to the ship builders strike,"

"You are nothing but a Freak. You do not have that power. No Freak should be allowed to have the power. You need to all be killed,"

A part of me wanted to laugh at this man. He was useless and pointless and utterly unneeded. It reminded me of when I pointed this out to the Queen. I remember her answer being something along the lines of *the Head of Military is a fun job to put people in if you want to execute them later.*

Continuing to smile, I wondered what mistake or thing this fool at said or done to the Queen to annoy her.

"Do not smile at me Freak and as for your Freak of a boyfriend..."

I didn't even let him finish the sentence.

I charged forward.

l the sweet fruits were overwhelming and
he couldn't wait for her mother to turn up
em all the scheming she had been up to in

well-armoured hand reached across the
grab a rather delicious looking piece of
 pie. Alessandria hit Nemesio's hand away.
 smiled at her playfully and she just stared
lmiring his beautiful strong jawline and the
s stunning face. His hair being perfectly
t only amplified his face. He was simply

ter their date, Alessandria wanted to be
That night was perfect. She could be a real
 once. Not a member of the Nobility or a
s Procurator. Just a girl with an attractive

t as much as she longed for Nemesio, there
thing stopping her. She just didn't know

n odd gentle draft made Alessandria turn to
o see her beautiful brother Daniel sitting
ning his dull blade so fast it was creating a
eeze.
lessandria bit her lip slightly. She had heard
niel's fight with the Head of the Military.
n't a problem in the slightest, the Family
would hardly suffer. But it was what he said
erned her.
he woman working for the Head of the
ad come to her after what happened. She
ear that people still thought the world was
 if Daniel was dead.

Diving on him.

He screamed.

The feeling of his fat flesh was disgusting.

I slammed his fists into his face.

The woman just stood there watching.

Waves of fat moved as I smashed my fists into him.

He tried to move.

I had him pinned.

His nose shattered.

Blood poured from his nose.

A set of heavy metal cladded footsteps pounded down the hall.

Thinking it was Alessandria, I jumped off the Head of the Military.

Looking with narrow eyes at the figure, I saw a tall ornate golden armoured warrior with an immense golden spear and shield in his hands.

His face was covered by an ornate golden mask of an angel.

"Guard! Kill him!" the Head of the Military shouted.

The Guard walked over him. Purposefully standing on his hand.

"Master Fireheart, your Mother has returned. She needs to speak with you. I have orders to take you there," the Guard said.

I nodded to the Guard and we started to walk away.

"Freak! I'm going to kill you and your

boyfriend,"

As I passed him, I kicked him in the head.
No one threatens the man I love.
No one!

CH

As Alessandria
pastries and the even
on the heavy smoo
excitement was building

It had been ove
her scheming, wonderfu
completely concerned
learnt something abou
mythical figure that had
the Triad. The even str
Queen dead.

But Alessandria
she reminded herself tha
a Dominicus Procurator

And there were
different shapes and
platters in front of her.
dinner table that looked
solid polished grey stor
probably have a party
there would still be room

Of course these people didn't know how many times Daniel had saved Ordericous from its enemies.

Looking at her brother in his typical black leather trench coat and trousers. Alessandria paused and looked at his right sleeve. It was turned back revealing some of Daniel's arm and the deep red scars from all those years ago.

He never showed even a piece of his arms in public.

Alessandria wanted to point it out to him but the sight of a minor fresh cut caught her eye.

A wave of pure... protectiveness washed over her. She wanted to lovingly talk to Daniel to make sure he was okay. She needed to support him. Alessandria wasn't going to let Daniel be alone and let him hurt himself this time.

He must have saw Alessandria looking at his sleeve as he unrolled it, covering up the exposed flesh, and smiled a little.

"I cut my arm on that foolish Head of the Military earlier. But thank you for being concerned. I do appreciate it," Daniel said.

Alessandria nodded. She let out a breath she didn't know she was holding. Alessandria really, really loved her brother.

The sound of massive heavy wooden doors screamed out and Kinaaz Fireheart walked through.

Alessandria smiled as she saw her mother walk in. Wearing her posh black silk robe with her thin golden armour underneath with her well-aged features glowing with renewed power and youth.

Alessandria and the other two shot up to greet her.

"Mother," Daniel said.

"Oh Daniel. It's wonderful to see you. and Alessandria you look so tall and grown up,"

"Mother, you've been gone a month, not years," Alessandria said.

"Alessandria always so picky on the details," Kinaaz said as she walked round to the other side of the table and picked up a bright red sugary pastry.

"I presume it is safe to say you enjoyed yourself,"

"Alessandria it was amazing. If I had known rehab would be like that. I would have gone years ago. It was wonderful. So many people to scheme against and take their secrets and money. Wow,"

Alessandria rolled her eyes at her mother. She was meant to be getting help for her drinking, not scheming against innocent people.

Nemesio looked at Alessandria and pointed towards a plate of tartlets.

She waved her hand dismissively at him.

He grabbed a few.

"Mother, what do you know about the Seeker?" Alessandria asked.

"Oh now that is a wonderful story. Well, I was playing poker against this terminally ill man. He's worth a fortune I tell you,"

Alessandria grabbed an iced finger. The sticky icing feeling strange on her fingers.

"And this ill man lost to me. But he wanted to keep playing. So I said to him if you want to keep playing then I want to know a secret that he was taking to the grave. He had mentioned it in passing,"

Daniel leaned forward.

Alessandria followed.

Diving on him.

He screamed.

The feeling of his fat flesh was disgusting.

I slammed his fists into his face.

The woman just stood there watching.

Waves of fat moved as I smashed my fists into him.

He tried to move.

I had him pinned.

His nose shattered.

Blood poured from his nose.

A set of heavy metal cladded footsteps pounded down the hall.

Thinking it was Alessandria, I jumped off the Head of the Military.

Looking with narrow eyes at the figure, I saw a tall ornate golden armoured warrior with an immense golden spear and shield in his hands.

His face was covered by an ornate golden mask of an angel.

"Guard! Kill him!" the Head of the Military shouted.

The Guard walked over him. Purposefully standing on his hand.

"Master Fireheart, your Mother has returned. She needs to speak with you. I have orders to take you there," the Guard said.

I nodded to the Guard and we started to walk away.

"Freak! I'm going to kill you and your

boyfriend,"

As I passed him, I kicked him in the head.
No one threatens the man I love.
No one!

CHAPTER 3

As Alessandria breathed in the sweet smelling pastries and the even sweeter fruits as she sat down on the heavy smooth brown oak chair. Her excitement was building.

It had been over a month since she had seen her scheming, wonderful mother. Of course, she was completely concerned by the fact her mother had learnt something about the Seeker. The strange mythical figure that had some strange connection to the Triad. The even stranger people who wanted the Queen dead.

But Alessandria informed those concerns as she reminded herself that she was a daughter first and a Dominicus Procurator second.

And there were some amazing pastries in all different shapes and sizes laid out on immense platters in front of her. As did a massive solid oak dinner table that looked right at home in the large solid polished grey stone chamber. That you could probably have a party of a hundred people in and there would still be room.

All the sweet fruits were overwhelming and amazing. She couldn't wait for her mother to turn up and tell them all the scheming she had been up to in rehab.

A well-armoured hand reached across the table to grab a rather delicious looking piece of strawberry pie. Alessandria hit Nemesio's hand away.

He smiled at her playfully and she just stared at him. Admiring his beautiful strong jawline and the rest of his stunning face. His hair being perfectly parted that only amplified his face. He was simply beautiful.

After their date, Alessandria wanted to be with him. That night was perfect. She could be a real person for once. Not a member of the Nobility or a Dominicus Procurator. Just a girl with an attractive man.

But as much as she longed for Nemesio, there was something stopping her. She just didn't know what.

An odd gentle draft made Alessandria turn to her left to see her beautiful brother Daniel sitting there spinning his dull blade so fast it was creating a bit of a breeze.

Alessandria bit her lip slightly. She had heard about Daniel's fight with the Head of the Military. That wasn't a problem in the slightest, the Family Business would hardly suffer. But it was what he said that concerned her.

The woman working for the Head of the Military had come to her after what happened. She hated to hear that people still thought the world was better off if Daniel was dead.

"So as always he lost to me. Silly man. Then he told me his secret. He knew a witch that went by the name Seeker up in the woods,"

Alessandria's eyes narrowed.

"We need to speak with this man," Nemesio said.

Kinaaz laughed. "Don't be silly. He died the day after and now all his money is mine,"

Alessandria rolled her eyes. Her Mother was scheming. She'll give her that.

"Did he tell you where he lives?" Daniel asked, as he grabbed his first pastry.

"Yes, it's near Old Dead Annie,"

"Isn't that that massive dead oak, ten miles away?" Nemesio asked.

Kinaaz nodded as she elegantly licked her fingers.

Whilst Alessandria wanted to stay and catch up with her mother, and maybe give her a lesson in morality, she knew she had bigger problems. She had to find the Seeker and learn about the Triad.

Standing up Alessandria gestured to Nemesio to go but he stared at the sweet pastries with wide eyes.

She rolled her eyes.

"Take some with you. It's 9am. That should last you til dinner," Alessandria said, walking off.

As her and Nemesio walked away, Alessandria heard Daniel asked why she was staring at me. Then she was a little concerned by Kinaaz's answer.

"Because Daniel, I've got a scheme to complete!"

CHAPTER 4

My eyes were fixed on the door as it slammed shut as Alessandria and Nemesio left the chamber, no doubt going to the stables to prepare the horses for the ten mile ride. Leaving me, Daniel Fireheart, here alone with my scheming mother.

Turning my head and judging the ugly grey stone walls and the even uglier grey polished floor. I looked back at the delicious brown oak table of pastries in front of me. Unlike my sister, I wasn't the biggest fan of all these unhealthy pastries but these were great.

Their sweet, fruity smell was brilliant and very refreshing. It was far better than that disgusting damp smell from that corridor with the Head of the Military.

My fingers still itched for a blade to kill him with. He was a horrid human and... I tried to force those thoughts out of my head. As much as I knew they were unhealthy, they were correct.

But an extremely rare wave of emotion washed over me as I thought about what Alessandria had thought. I didn't know she cared that much about me. She didn't know it but I saw the look on her face when she saw that cut, and she wanted to protect me.

Now that was the sister I loved.

Feeling my dull blade spin slowly in my hand, I looked at mother smiling at me as she ate another bright green tartlet. It did look good. My mouth felt as if it was already tasting the sour green berries in it.

I really did want one but I forced myself to focus on mother. What was she scheming? Or more importantly, why did she need my help?

It was probably just because I'm dating Harrison and she wanted access to the Queen's Engineering department. I really wish Harrison was here. I would love to see his beautiful youthful face and that stunning blond hair parted so perfectly to the left.

The sound of mother licking her fingers drew my attention back to her.

"What scheme are you planning?" Daniel asked.

"Daniel, we haven't seen each other in over a month. I hear there's lots to talk about,"

"We never *just talk*,"

"Yes we do. I've always spoken to you. You always helped me scheming,"

"Yes, scheming Mother. Not just talking. Not just seeing how I am," I said, unrolling up a piece of my sleeve. Revealing a few centimetres of my deep cuts.

She looked at my arm quickly then… it was like something changed in her. Mother looked around and when presumably she knew we were alone. Her

Of course these people didn't know how many times Daniel had saved Ordericous from its enemies.

Looking at her brother in his typical black leather trench coat and trousers. Alessandria paused and looked at his right sleeve. It was turned back revealing some of Daniel's arm and the deep red scars from all those years ago.

He never showed even a piece of his arms in public.

Alessandria wanted to point it out to him but the sight of a minor fresh cut caught her eye.

A wave of pure... protectiveness washed over her. She wanted to lovingly talk to Daniel to make sure he was okay. She needed to support him. Alessandria wasn't going to let Daniel be alone and let him hurt himself this time.

He must have saw Alessandria looking at his sleeve as he unrolled it, covering up the exposed flesh, and smiled a little.

"I cut my arm on that foolish Head of the Military earlier. But thank you for being concerned. I do appreciate it," Daniel said.

Alessandria nodded. She let out a breath she didn't know she was holding. Alessandria really, really loved her brother.

The sound of massive heavy wooden doors screamed out and Kinaaz Fireheart walked through.

Alessandria smiled as she saw her mother walk in. Wearing her posh black silk robe with her thin golden armour underneath with her well-aged features glowing with renewed power and youth.

Alessandria and the other two shot up to greet her.

"Mother," Daniel said.

"Oh Daniel. It's wonderful to see you. and Alessandria you look so tall and grown up,"

"Mother, you've been gone a month, not years," Alessandria said.

"Alessandria always so picky on the details," Kinaaz said as she walked round to the other side of the table and picked up a bright red sugary pastry.

"I presume it is safe to say you enjoyed yourself,"

"Alessandria it was amazing. If I had known rehab would be like that. I would have gone years ago. It was wonderful. So many people to scheme against and take their secrets and money. Wow,"

Alessandria rolled her eyes at her mother. She was meant to be getting help for her drinking, not scheming against innocent people.

Nemesio looked at Alessandria and pointed towards a plate of tartlets.

She waved her hand dismissively at him.

He grabbed a few.

"Mother, what do you know about the Seeker?" Alessandria asked.

"Oh now that is a wonderful story. Well, I was playing poker against this terminally ill man. He's worth a fortune I tell you,"

Alessandria grabbed an iced finger. The sticky icing feeling strange on her fingers.

"And this ill man lost to me. But he wanted to keep playing. So I said to him if you want to keep playing then I want to know a secret that he was taking to the grave. He had mentioned it in passing,"

Daniel leaned forward.

Alessandria followed.

face changed to be calmer, gentler but more loving.

Mother reached across the table to grab my hand.

I didn't take it.

"We suffered a lot because of Justin, didn't we?" Mother said.

I couldn't disagree with her. My thankfully dead brother Justin was far, far worse than any criminal Alessandria had ever dealt with. The memories of him beating me almost to death danced across my mind. Then the memories of seeing him beat Mother to stop him from hurting Alessandria also showed up.

"Daniel, I do love you. Which is why I'm scheming,"

Now she had my attention.

"I think that's the first time you've said that,"

Her eyes dropped to the floor for a moment.

"It is true. I am sorry I wasn't around for the past few years. There's a lot I keep from you and Alessandria. People want us destroyed,"

"Hence the scheming?" I asked.

"It keeps us alive. It stops people from acting on their threats,"

"Why did you choose the rehab facility you did? I suggested some better places for you,"

"I know Daniel but they didn't have a former Inquisitorial Servant,"

My dull blade spun faster.

As we were clearly going to be talking about

that horrific organisation, I definitely needed a pastry. I reached over and picked up a delicious cream filled choux bun that felt soft in my hand.

I bit into it. My mouth exploding with delicious sweet creamy flavours.

"Why do you want to talk to a former Servant?" I asked.

"Because he knew things about a certain Order of the Inquisition that we need,"

"Wait, you're going to help me and Alessandria convince the Nobility and Inquisition to change the law?"

She quickly nodded.

Part of me couldn't believe it. Especially when she said that changing the law to allow gays to be Lord of Noble Houses was ridiculous. What changed her mind?

"Your progress surprised me. I obviously raised two great children. It's a defeat getting all but one Noble House so far pledged to your cause,"

I know she meant it as a compliment but concern grew in me. Mainly at the thought of still having four Inquisitorial Orders, the House of Blueheart and the Church to convince. So many vital pieces still left.

"How are you going to help?"

"Daniel, the Servant told me he kept tabs on the Order of the Blessed Earth and there's a target proving elusive to them,"

I really hoped she wasn't thinking what I

think she was.

    Mother reached for another bright red tartlet.

    "So, we're going to catch him for them,"

    And she was.

    As much as I admired my Mother's courage, did she really think an Order of the Inquisition would take it well that some Nobles captured a prisoner were they failed?

    Also the Order of the Blessed Earth weren't exactly known for their kindness towards the Nobility. Especially, as they blame the nobility for attacking the ground and ripping out its organs. (I presume it's talking about the minerals and jewels, but who knows with these Inquisitors)

    "You aren't convinced?" Mother asked.

    "Well Harrison's working so I haven't got anything better to do,"

    "Excellent, I'll order my personal war gear to be prepared. This will be great. Fighting side by side with my son!"

    A part of me really felt as if I was going to regret this!

CHAPTER 5

With boiling heat in the stables made Alessandria wipe the sweat off her forehead. This was not her idea of fun. Preparing horses inside this little brown wooden stable with four horse pens was ridiculous. It was basically a greenhouse.

Stretching her neck slightly, Alessandria almost gagged as she looked around the stables and smelt the horses and brown organic material in the pens. This is definitely why stable boys prepare the horses.

Alessandria could even feel the heat from the ground seep into her boots. This was the last time she was going to let Nemesio choose what they did next.

She had wanted to go to the library to pick up a little book she knew on magic users. But Nemesio had decided against that and that time was of the essence. She agreed, but time was useless if they were killed by a magic fireball!

Looking over at Nemesio, she had to admire his smooth elegant movements as he stroked his massive horse and prepared it for the journey ahead. Then Alessandria couldn't help herself by admiring the way his hair looked smooth and lifeful despite the heat.

She really wished her hair looked like that.

The sound of her horse sneezing reminded Alessandria that her horse was already and wanting to go.

She couldn't blame the horse. It was ridiculously hot. Normally, all the Royal and Fireheart horses would be moved up to the fields in the daytime. But these two had been given gallons of cold water in their pens in case they were needed. Thankfully they were needed.

Alessandria hated the idea of these beautiful horses being stuck in a pen all day just in case. Maybe she should get that changed somehow.

As she was done Alessandria simply stood there gently stroking the mane of her handsome horse. The horse hair feeling wiry between her fingers. And she focused on Nemesio who was still doing god knows what with his horse.

Casting her mind back she knew it had been a month since their date and she loved it. For the first time (probably ever) she had been able to relax, be herself and just talk about whatever. Instead of always having to think before she spoke in public or it might reflect badly on her House.

Then Nemesio had told her about his life and what he had had to do for the Inquisition just to survive. It… It troubled her.

She didn't know why but there was something else that stopped her from getting too close to Nemesio. She just needed to find out what.

She watched him as he stretched his beautiful back highlighting his muscles and Nemesio wandered over to Alessandria with his horse.

"Are you ready to go?" he said.

"I'm the one who was waiting for you,"

Nemesio nodded. "Do you know about this massive old oak?"

Alessandria smiled for a moment as she remembered playing on the branches and jumping off them as a child with some friends.

"Not a lot. It's largely an old folk tale. A massive tree with so-called powers and magical creatures living inside it," Alessandria said.

"Nonsense?"

"Nemesio, I can't believe a former Inquisitor hasn't encountered magical beings before,"

"True but we're Inquisitors. We kill all those who oppose us,"

Alessandria knew he was being honest and tried to say it as a joke. Yet a memory of their date came into her mind. The time when Nemesio had told her of when he had slaughtered an entire village of innocent witches for opposing a possible threat to the former King.

The Inquisition and the Queen's father were ridiculous in their fearful behaviour. Something Alessandria was not going to let other people do. Hence, the need to keep the righteous Queen on the throne, no matter the cost.

Whilst Nemesio jumped on his horse, Alessandria saw him look at something behind her. Turning around Alessandria smiled a little as she saw

Harrison's rather pleasing slightly muscular frame and his pleasantly thick blond hair. She knew Harrison was dating her brother, but a woman could dream. And in all honesty she was happy for Daniel to find such a beautiful man.

Then a part of her felt immense guilt for even remotely admiring Harrison, but she really wanted to look at Nemesio. Alessandria needed to sort out these feelings but she had a much more important job to do first.

"Alexis, can I talk to you for a moment?" Harrison asked.

"Ride ahead Nemesio. I'll catch up,"

"Really? I'm too quick for you,"

"Go. I'm riding a Fireheart horse. Very fast. Now go. I must talk to Harrison,"

Seeing Nemesio and his horse thunder off out of the stable, Alessandria turned back to Harrison.

"Have you seen Daniel at all?" Harrison asked.

"No, not really. I saw him earlier in passing. Why?"

Harrison paused.

"Harrison, Daniel loves you and you are basically family. You can talk to me,"

"It's just that Danny hasn't been home for about a week and it feels like he's been avoiding me,"

Alessandria cocked her head.

Now it wasn't that she didn't believe Harrison but Daniel was devoted to Harrison. The idea of

Daniel avoiding Harrison seemed farfetched at best.

"I saw Daniel the other day. Maybe five days ago and he was talking about you constantly. Saying how great you were," Alessandria said.

Harrison smiled at that.

"I know he's been busy preparing a project and to meet the new Head of the Military. Maybe it's that. Just remember that Daniel loves you more than anything,"

Harrison nodded.

"If I see him, I'll tell him you want to see him. I think we both know autism can make people a little fixated on a project," Alessandria said.

"Thank you. I know I'm probably being silly but thank you," Harrison said before walking away.

Alessandria knew her horse made a sound but she just stood there for a moment. This wasn't right. She hadn't lied when she said Daniel was devoted to Harrison. Yet Daniel would never avoid Harrison. Not after what happened to them, and the years together they missed out on.

Whatever was going on, Alessandria would find out. That was a promise. This time she would protect her brother.

CHAPTER 6

Well, when dear Mother told me, Daniel Fireheart, we were going to a village on the outskirts of Ordericous, I wasn't quite expecting this place.

It was impossible not to judge this place as I tied up my horse to a large wooden pole at the entrance of the village.

Looking around I saw thick mud covering the ground and the twenty wooden round huts with their domed thatch roofs littered the village with a chaotic pattern. It was almost like someone decided to throw up huts and see where they landed.

It was hardly attractive so I suppose there was no better hideout for a target of the Inquisition.

Multiple men and women covered in muddy clothes walked about chatting and doing their daily business. Well, I say walking- they were strolling about pointlessly. I hate it when people do that. Either you walk with purpose or you don't walk at all. Or that's just the autism in me talking. I love structure and purpose.

My dull blade spun slower in my hand as I looked at all the people. Trying to weigh up who was the target.

The smell of dirt, pigs and faecal matter made me cover my nose with a piece of my leather trench coat. The smooth warm leather feeling calming against my skin.

A gentle breeze making the tree branches smash into each other made a part of me grateful for being in the forest. At least it was cool and pleasant. Probably the only problem of always wearing a leather trench coat and trousers were they did get very hot in the summer.

The sight of mother in her full sterile white and gold body armour that presented her as some angelic divine being from an ancient story made me smile. She definitely knew how to make an impression. It was only amplified by her stunning white cloak.

Taking a few steps forward, feeling the soft mud moving under my feet, I walked further into the village.

I heard mother walk behind me. My dulled blade turning slowly in my hand.

"I'm surprised you haven't mentioned Harrison to me. Granted I am a little surprised you ended up with *that* boy," Mother said.

I smiled. "Mother that is why me and Alessandria did not tell you. How dare I date a commoner and mess up your schemes,"

Feeling her metal cladded fingers softly touch my arm, I took a deep breath. I really hated being touched.

"Daniel, I know even you and Alessandria think of me as some witch who is only concerned with scheming. But I am your mother first and foremost. You are happy. That is what is important to me,"

I waited.

"But I did have a perfect Nobleman lined up for you,"

"Mother you do remember what happened two months ago when you first arranged a gay marriage for me? Our Castle got destroyed,"

She let go of my arm and gave me a quick kiss on the cheek. Before walking a few steps in front of me.

A part of me felt some strange emotion pulse through me. That was probably the first time she had given me true affection in recent years since father died.

But another part of me really wanted to see Harrison and admire his perfect face and body.

Seeing that mother had stopped a few metres away, I stepped through dark smelly mud to reach her.

"See that Daniel. That's our target," Mother said.

Following her glaze, I looked at passed a crowd of dirty peasants and multiple tall wooden huts. To see a strong, muscular old man wearing a bright red uniform. But he had two massive long swords in his hands.

The target started to walk towards the crowd of people.

We slowly walked over too.

"Are we going to kill him?" I asked.

"No, we need him alive,"

"You know there are at least five Inquisitors here,"

Mother looked puzzled at me briefly.

"Two behind us. Two to our left. One behind the target,"

Mother nodded her head and stopped for a moment.

"Good job," she said.

A shot screamed through the air.

People screamed and shouted.

Five men charged forward.

Two dashed past us.

They all had bright green metal armour covered with leaves and bright red blood.

Their swords were massive and thick.

These men screamed out something about honour to the Goddess of Nature.

The Inquisition was here to slaughter.

In the crowd people screamed as the target charged forward.

He slashed and lashed at the chests and throats of the crowd.

Their blood sprayed.

The inquisition charged in.

Sounds of immense metal clanging and smashing into each other echoed everywhere.

I whipped out my swords.

I charged in.

One man screamed.

I looked up.

A head of an Inquisitor was shattered as his lifeless body thumped onto the ground.

Something threw me to the ground.

Someone slammed their fists into my face.

Pain flooded my body.

My vision cleared.

Another Inquisitor was on me.

I struggled.

The Inquisitor kept smashing his fists into me.

Air rushed past.

Blood poured onto my face.

The Inquisitor's lifeless corpse fell to the ground.

Mother's sword dripped blood.

She helped me up.

More screams came as more Inquisitors were slaughtered.

Their bodies stabbed, lashed and shattered.

The target was some demonic gymnastic as he jumped up. Dodging every attack.

Blue fireballs rained down upon the village.

People from behind screamed in agony.

We spun around.

Three women in black cloaks stormed in.

Witches!

Unleashing immense blue fireballs at innocent people.

The huts roared as the fires consumed them.

I charged.

Air crackled with magical energy.

Bright blue lightning rods shot out of one woman's hand.

I dodged.

Mother charged in.

The lightning hit her.

Nothing happened.

The witches paused.

All three witches launched a torrent of immense black fire.

The fire laughed and crackled.

Whatever it touched turned to ash.

The fire came towards us.

Mother grabbed me.

Throwing me to the ground.

Using her massive white armour to shield us.

I felt mother's breath wet on my neck.

She shook.

The flames rushed over us.

Mother screamed.

She whispered words I didn't understand.

Then nothing.

Forcing herself off me, Mother gingerly stood up and she pointed towards the three witches riding away on shadowy black horses.

When she turned around, I wanted to gasp as I saw her back armour was reduced to nothing and all I could see was her well-aged bare back.

Although, I thought I could see the rest of her armour glow briefly before it went out.

Looking at the rest of the village, all I could see were the charred remains of a former village.

There were no more huts nor people.

Only the charred, smouldering remains of corpses remained. Including the smouldering fragments of green Inquisitorial armour and the red uniform of the target.

CHAPTER 7

Pulling on the black smooth reins of her impressive horse, Alessandria and her horse slowed to a gentle stroll as they rode towards Old Dead Annie.

Alessandria felt her horse move strangely as the rough root covered ground of the forest made the horse tread on uneven ground.

A cool refreshing breeze blew past making Alessandria felt good after the hard ten mile ride here.

The lust thick green trees and their immense branches covered most of the canopy. Allowing only the smallest rays of direct sunlight to shine through like rods of holy light.

Thankfully, despite it being slightly dark. Alessandria could see almost everything around her. From the thick trees with their rough bark to the uneven and outright dangerous ground with twisted roots and branches that could and probably would kill you.

Alessandria rolled her eyes as she realised a ten mile ride on a Fireheart horse should have taken 15 minutes. But fighting through a mile of this thick overgrown forest made the journey take an hour.

Not good when the Queen's life when depended on it.

The smell of bitter smoke faintly filled the air as did the damp refreshing smell of the forest.

A wave of calm and relaxation washed over Alessandria.

As her horse stepped over a large root and turned slightly, Alessandria saw the beautiful tree. Old Dead Annie was a beast of an oak tree with its trunk tens of metres thick and covered in thick shiny sap that was meant to have healing powers. But Alessandria doubted this.

Looking up she was filled with wonder as Alessandria could barely see where the branches began. Let alone where the tree stopped.

Just looking at it, pure awe pulsed through her. There was amazing and so specular about looking at this immense tree.

Whilst she had absolutely no idea why the tree was called Old Dead Annie. Her mind casted back to some fairy tale about a woman who ran away from her Master and prayed to be with the Goddess of Nature. She prayed for 80 days and 80 nights sitting on the stump of an Oak tree. Apparently only being sustained by her faith.

Then on the 81st day, the Goddess rewarded her by growing the stump around her. Killing her so the Goddess could claim her.

Alessandria didn't know if the story was wise or pointless but at least Annie, or whatever the girl's true name was, got what she wanted.

A thump came from behind her.

Tapping her horse to continue, Alessandria quickly turned her head to see Nemesio's horse abandon him as it ran back the way it came. Nemesio walked behind her.

She could hardly blame the horse. These roots and this horrific terrain were hardly horse material. It was a miracle even a Fireheart horse had made it this far.

A part of her wanted to ask Nemesio to hop on her horse so badly. Allowing him to wrap his strong arms around her and she would ride with him like a couple. Or just friends. But at least she could be close to him.

She shook her head.

The thought of Daniel and Harrison came to her mind. They both loved each other so much and they were perfectly happy. She wanted that. She really wanted that.

But she knew she'd be lying if she didn't say she was worried about Daniel. So many what-ifs were going through her mind.

Taking a deep breath she promised herself she would find what was going on with the Seeker. Then she would talk to Daniel.

The sound of a massive wooden stick whacking branches made Alessandria smile and focus on the present.

Looking towards Old Dead Annie, Alessandria had to smile as she saw Hellen whacking some branches away from her. Alessandria didn't understand how even through all the uneven and muddy ground, Hellen's grey Procurator coat looked fine and *even* freshly ironed.

Climbing off her horse, Alessandria mockingly rubbed Nemesio's back for his failure to maintain his horse and looked towards Hellen.

"Ya two are late. I got here ages ago," Hellen said.

"We are not late. You are early. How did you get here so fast?" Alessandria asked.

"I walked through the forest. I didn't waste ma time riding some horse. I mean just look at this ground,"

Alessandria nodded. Hellen did have a point.

Feeling a gentle breeze blew her hair, Alessandria turned to face the immense tree. Part in amazement. Part in fear. What was so important about this tree?

"So why ya bring us here Alexis?"

"My mother didn't make the clearest of sense. Either someone lives here who knows the Seeker or the Seeker lives here,"

"And it didn't occur to ya to bring armed men if the Seeker lives here?"

"That what's your massive stick is for,"

Hellen nodded as if it was a stupid question.

Little whispers echoed around the forest.

The branches creeped.

Alessandria turned.

She looked up.

Hundreds of little glowing lights descended on from the treetops.

"What are they?" Nemesio asked.

"Fairies," Alessandria said.

As the lights got closer tiny little elegant bodies of blue light could be seen.

Alessandria tensed.

She knew fairies were extremely dangerous.

Thankfully the city smoke was toxic to them.

Yet there was sadly no smoke here.

The little fairies smiled.

Showing tens of microscopic dagger like teeth.

Alessandria saw Nemesio smile.

He must have dealt with these creatures before.

The fairies stopped. Pointing behind them.

A twig snapped.

Alessandria turned.

Three women in black cloaks appeared.

The air hummed with magical energy.

Alessandria's hair went static.

Her stomach churned.

The women whipped out their hands.

Alessandria went flying.

She smashed into a massive tree.

Her back ached.

Hellen landed on top of her.

Alessandria jumped back up.

She saw Nemesio charge at the women.

They muttered something.

Nemesio's sword glowed bright red.

He screamed.

Smoke poured from his hand.

He dropped his sword.

The women launched a fireball at him.

He dodged.

Alessandria charged over.

The women saw her.

A vine wrapped around her ankle.

Alessandria fell to the ground.

Cutting her head on a massive root.

She heard multiple vines being whacked to death by Hellen's massive wooden stick.

The fairies advanced.

They crawled all over Alessandria.

She rapidly whacked them off.

Her ears were filled with their laughter.

Blood dripped down her cheeks and legs as the fairies bit into her flesh.

She screamed.

She needed Daniel.

She needed someone to save her.

An immense deafening crackling came from the forest. Everyone stopped. Alessandria stood up. The Fairies backed away. Everyone looked at Old Dead Annie.

The ancient oak twisted and snapped.

Its trunk split.

A young woman made from wood charged out.

The black cloaked women roared with rage.

The air hummed loudly with magical energy.

Alessandria rushed over to Nemesio and Hellen.

They all rushed over to the side.

The three women launched a torrent of black fire at the wooden woman.

The wooden woman laughed.

Deflecting it.

The black cloaked witches were thrown to the floor.

The wooden woman ran over to Alessandria.

"Come with me. Now!"

The wooden woman rushed off into the forest. Waving Alessandria and her friends to follow her.

She looked at the three witches.

They were recovering.
Alessandria grabbed Hellen and Nemesio and ran.
"What's your name?" Alessandria asked.
"Annie,"

CHAPTER 8

My arms burned and my body became increasingly hot as we walked across the stone bridge to the Inquisitorial Fortress.

Making myself forget, or attempt to at least, that I, Daniel Fireheart, and my scheming mother were about to walk into a place that hated us. I made myself focus on the details.

Feeling the rough cobblestones under my leather booted feet and the bright midnight sun beam down on me. I was partially rethinking my choice of clothing. Summer really really wasn't the time of year to be wearing a leather trench coat.

The smell of bitter scented smoke and the sound of people chatting inside the immense fortress made me look at it. My hate built within and my dulled blade spun quickly.

This fortress with its spiky stone walls made from massive blocks of stone was a disgrace. Everything about these people were disgraceful.

Even the gates we were approaching were stupid. They were tens of metres tall made from solid gold and wrapped with vines dripping poison.

As if gold was practical if this was attacked.

In fact, I would love for this fortress to be attacked after what the Inquisitors to me.

Taking a deep breath, I forced the memories of my torture sessions away and I focused on the sound of the chatting and the flowing moat under the bridge.

Turning around quickly, I had to admit that this was a good place for a fortress. (At least this Inquisitorial Order wasn't that pointless and dumb) With tall hills and thick forest allowing the defenders to see for miles. And the forest was cut back in such a way that it became impassable.

At least their Goddess of Nature could thrive. It was a shame these Inquisitors didn't let gays or any other abominations thrive.

As we got closer to these silly gates, a little side door opened out of one of the immense towers either side of the gate. Revealing four heavily armed guards dressed in thick bright green armour and holding two staffs each. Ready to hurt us.

I really wasn't afraid of some Inquisitors.

My family had got an entire Order burned before. If the need arose this time would be no different.

I know Alessandria would love to abolish the Inquisition. If only to keep me and Harrison (my beautiful boy) safe.

The guard raised a hand to stop us as a strong, tall lady, maybe in her late thirties, marched out of the Fortress. Dressed in some ridiculous white, jewelled ceremonial robes and holding a golden staff with some green orb on the top.

In other words, just Inquisition silliness.

Although, I did like how she braided her strong long brown hair with metres of red vine. That looked cool.

Mother stepped forward. Thankfully, we had stopped off at the Castle first to get her a change of clothes. I was not going to walk about Ordericous with Mother if she was walking around with a naked back.

Thankfully, she was now wearing a long posh light green dress with a necklace with a piece of an amber covered leaf in the middle.

I suppose it was good she was trying to be civil to this Order.

Personally, I wouldn't have bothered.

The woman in her ceremonial robes stopped a few metres from us. She was clearly the Inquisitorial Saga for this forsaken Order.

As badly as I wanted to unleash my Flesheater ability and slaughter her. I allowed Mother to lead.

"Mighty Saga of the Order of the Blessed Earth-" Mother said.

The Saga interrupted. "Lady Kinaaz Fireheart it is an honour. I have heard such great things about you and your mind. You are impressive for a Keeper of the Unholy,"

She looked at me.

"Dear Master Daniel, you are unholy but please rest assured you can be saved. The Goddess of Nature can heal you. She can banish the demons from-"

I whipped out my sword and pointed it at her throat.

The Guards went to charge.

The Saga raised a hand to stop them.

"Dearest Saga, I have seen what you do in your foul Goddess' name. Tell my mother what you did to my childhood best friend!"

The Saga only smiled.

Mother didn't do anything.

"Samic O'Fish that was his name. He was the first person I told I was gay. He helped me accept myself. And you slaughtered him," I said.

The Saga's smile grew.

"He was my best friend. What did he do wrong? He wasn't gay. He wasn't an abomination. Why!" I shouted.

The Saga started laughing.

"Was it because you couldn't come after me? So you went after my best friend?"

"Dearest Master Fireheart, I killed him myself. He wasn't gay but he was a criminal. He helped gays. He concluded with the demons that made you gay. He corrupted you. He forsaken the Goddess,"

I so, so badly wanted to kill her.

She murdered by best friend. The boy who helped me before I had properly met Harrison. He was just trying to help me and this… woman killed him.

Feeling Mother's eyes burn into my side, I forced myself to put my sword away.

"You see Master Fireheart, there is still hope for you. So please come inside and let the Goddess heal you,"

"I will not be going inside your disgraceful Fortress. I will burn it to the ground before that!"

"And I would die before I let you take my Son," Mother said.

I threw a charred shard of green armour at the Saga.

She threw it.

Her eyes widened. Filling with pain. Probably the thought of one of her own dying.

Mother's eyes narrowed. "We did not do this. Three witches attacked us and the Inquisitors. We want to make a deal,"

The Guards around the Saga looked at each other. Unsure of what to do, their Saga was clearly in great pain at the loss. Not that I cared.

It was good she was suffering. At least she would feel a tiny amount of what I felt. I really miss Harrison. I wanted to go to him and relax in his arms but I had a job to do first.

The Saga wiped her eyes. "Lady Fireheart what sort of deal?"

"A bargain. We killed these witches working for the Seeker. In exchange. You pledge your Order's support for my daughter's law change,"

"Over my dead body!"

"That can be arranged!" I shouted.

"My Order will not help abominations. The

Goddess-"

"Your Goddess cannot help you when I release my leverage to the public," Mother said.

The Saga paused.

"There is no leverage. I am Pure. I am One with the Goddess,"

"Is the Goddess one with boys of the night?" Mother asked.

One of the guards smiled.

I had to agree.

"Your terms, Lady Fireheart?"

"It's simple really. We kill the witches and the Seeker. Avenging your losses. You pledge on the Goddess' life and your own that you will support my Daughter's law change in court."

"That is outrageous!" the Saga shouted.

I rolled my eyes.

"Or I will find these witches and tell them where YOU are? Three witches who love to kill Inquisitors. Imagine their excitement at killing a Saga," I said coldly.

The Saga paused. She looked around at her guards. The orb on top of her staff pulsing something.

She looked at Mother. "Fine, we agree to your terms. On our honour, the life of the... Goddess and ourselves. We will support Alessandria Fireheart's law change,"

I smiled a little. That must have killed her to say it. Whatever happens with their pledge and bargain, I would kill this Saga. No one kills a friend of mine and gets to live.

The sound of horses thundered behind us.

We turned around to see a tall man dressed in golden armour. I cocked my head at the sight of a Royal Guard.

"Lady and Master Fireheart, the Queen must see you. It's urgent,"

CHAPTER 9

Slowly coming to a stop, Alessandria paused to catch her breath. She had no idea how difficult it was to run through an uneven forest filled with massive trees and even thicker roots.

Whilst her body continued to take long very deep breaths, she looked behind her back into the thick trees with their spider like roots. She had almost snapped her ankle multiple times. Alessandria definitely knew she wasn't coming back here any time soon.

Returning her attention to what was in front of her, she wearily looked at this peaceful looking opening. It was only a few metres squared but after running through the forest. It was perfect.

Feeling the thick lustrous grass under her boots and breathing in the fresh dry air was perfect. Nothing like the thick damp air like of the forest.

The smell of honey came from somewhere too but Alessandria knew she didn't have long to savour these moments of peace. She knew the witches would be hunting them.

The little opening in amongst the forest reminded her of her childhood. And a particularly fun night she had as a teenager. She definitely knew how soft thick grass can be.

Looking back over to Nemesio and Hellen, Alessandria wanted to laugh at Hellen at inspecting her massive wooden stick. Checking it for marks and dents. Hellen must have found some because she gave her stick a massive smile.

And Alessandria had to conclude that Hellen was weird. Her best friend. But weird.

Then Nemesio wandered over to her. He was so close Alessandria could feel his body warmth and admire his impressive muscles that his armour highlighted so well.

She forced the thoughts away as she stared at the wooden woman. Alessandria didn't know whether to be amazed or horrified that a person could be made of wood. It wasn't natural. Her mind tried to understand it but all Alessandria could do was stare at the woman.

Acknowledging Annie's smooth wooden features and skin. Her long arms and legs wearing some strange tunic made from large oval leaves. Whatever this woman was she was powerful. But... she had almost killed those witches with ease.

A drop of fearful sweat dripped down her back as Alessandria wondered if they had traded one set of killers for another.

"What do you make of our new ally?" Nemesio asked.

"I would not want to be left alone," Alessandria said.

Turning around she saw Annie standing right behind them.

"I can assure you Lady Fireheart you are rather safe with me for the Goddess Wills it," Annie said.

Alessandria's eyes widened as she realised despite this woman being made from solid wood. She could speak perfect Ordericousian.

"The Goddess Wills it missy?" Hellen asked.

"Yes Lady of the Stick. The Goddess knows all and she demanded me to help you. Or save you from those Agents of the Seeker,"

"We were sent here to find you," Alessandria said.

"What?" Nemesio asked.

"Nemesio think about it. We were sent here to find a person who lived near Old Dead Annie to learn more,"

Nemesio nodded.

Hellen looked at her stick. "Is my stick made from a person?"

Alessandria rolled her eyes.

"No Lady of the Stick. Your stick is just wood,"

Hellen looked at her stick and nodded. "Of course, silly question. Ya can't whack people with people,"

Standing in front of Hellen to make sure she didn't say any more silly things to Annie. Alessandria looked at the wooden woman.

"What can you tell us about the Seeker?"

Tree branches snapped.

Everyone looked to the way they came.

Nothing.

More trees and twigs snapped.

"What can you-"

"Lady Fireheart I cannot tell you anything. The Goddess-"

"Damn ya Goddess. There are real people here. Lives are in danger. Why can't ya Goddess help us?"

Alessandria saw shadows move.

Entire branches in the distance shattered.

The smell of harsh bitter smoke filled the air.

"Hellen!" Alessandria shouted with authority.

Hellen reflexed up her massive stick. Ready to whack Annie.

"We are not your enemy but the lives of the people we protect depend on us finding the Seeker. Please help us," Alessandria said.

Roars of flames and fireballs echoed around the forest.

A volley of fireballs screamed through the air.

Alessandria jumped to the side.

She jumped up. She saw the three witches storming towards them.

The humming loudly with magical energy.

Alessandria saw Annie force herself up and stare with hate at these disgraceful witches.

Annie frowned. "Fine, as the Goddess Wills it. There is a waterfall. Two miles away. The forest is clearer. Easer to run through. There is a woman there who can help you. She knows everything,"

Nemesio moaned as he dodged a fireball.

Hellen whacked vines as they attacked her.

"Lady Alessandria, go. I will hold them off,"

Alessandria was not going to argue.

The air buzzed and crackled with golden magical energy as the vines were annihilated.

Alessandria grabbed Hellen and Nemesio and forced them towards the waterfall.

They broke out into a run.

Quickly looking behind her. Alessandria saw explosions of magical energy as Annie sacrificed herself for them.

She might not have believed in her so-called Goddess, but one innocent person had sacrificed themselves for their mission. Alessandria swore to keep that number there.

CHAPTER 10

Stepping into the grand meeting chamber of the Castle, I let out a little gasp of surprise as I looked at the stunning gold painted stone walls. As well as the large golden chandelier that hung from the hand painted ceiling. Showing something that I didn't fully understand. All I knew was there were a lot of blue swirls.

Lowering my glaze I smiled at the massive gold leafed round table in the centre of the chamber with three plain brown wooden chairs. In my head, it sounded so simple but in reality it was a stunning contrast to golden walls and table.

This contrast was amplified further by the polished black stone floor.

The sweetly scented incense burning in the two farthest corners were another good trick.

As I slowly spun my dulled blade in my hand, a part of me had to congratulate the Queen on making a statement. Granted I had no idea what statement she was trying to make. But judging how mother was walking inspecting the chamber. I think the statement was perfectly clear to 'normal' people.

Yet I also liked that you couldn't hear any of the castle staff walking around or chatting. Some of them could be so loud! Definitely something I hated with my heightened senses.

The sound of Mother pulling out a chair and inspecting underneath the table made me shake my head at her. What was she doing?

In all honesty, my mind casted back to the fact that the Queen had summoned us. She never did that. Of course, she might summon Alessandria for a mission or myself for something military related. But my mother?

I'm not even sure if my Mother and the Queen had met properly.

The distant sound of loud footsteps made me tense and spin my dulled blade a little faster.

I was attempted to warn Mother, but Where's the fun in that?

The sound of the doors opening and the loud footsteps of some attractive male guards made Mother shot up. Hitting her head on the table.

Then the Queen in a great white silky dress walked in. Smiling at Mother.

She regally waved the guards away and Guards shut the doors behind her.

It was only as she was walking towards the chairs that I realised her dress was layered with diamonds and gold threads.

Nothing about this meeting was subtle.

After the Queen sat down and elegantly sat with her soft youthful hands on her lap. Me and Mother joined her at the table.

A teapot and three perfectly filled teacups appeared filled with bright orange tea that filled the air with sweet lemon scents.

Again I had to smile at it all. The Queen knew how to impress with her limited magical tricks.

"Lady Fireheart, Master Fireheart I must thank you for finding the time to join me in this most pressing meeting," the Queen said.

"Your majesty as Lady Fireheart I must express my annoyance at being summoned like your common subjects,"

"I understand your frustration and please allow me to extend my deepest apologies. I do not treat the House of Fireheart as commoners,"

I was trying my hardest not to laugh at this battle of words.

"That is good to know your Majesty. But as you know my House is busy serving you so I politely ask for you to get to your point,"

"Of course and once again my deepest apologies. I spent my days talking to noblemen and noblewomen who are mostly clueless about most things so *I'm sure talking to you wouldn't be any different,*"

I busted out laughing as did the Queen.

Mother frowned.

"Your majesty please tell me why you bought us here,"

"My dearest Lady Fireheart, I wanted to see if you were still insecure about your House,"

"She is," I said.

"I can see that Master Fireheart and I must stress to your Ladyship that as long as I am on the throne. Your House will be protected at almost any cost. Your House is a great friend of the throne. And I protect my friends. Hence why I reversed many of the decisions my late Father made,"

After Mother seemed to regain some of her lady-ness, she smiled and elegantly drank some tea.

"Of course and the House of Fireheart thanks you for that almighty gesture. My Daughter Lady Alessandria tells me that caused you to make many enemies helping my son,"

The Queen looked at me. "It was worth it,"

I nodded my thanks to her.

"Now I must explain why I have most urgently summoned you here my Lady Fireheart. My agents inform me you are hunting the one they call the Seeker. As well as you have made a bargain with the Order of the Blessed Earth,"

"You are well informed your Majesty," Mother said.

"I am Queen. I must be well-informed. Thus, I need you to help me,"

"Of course, your majesty. Whatever you need?" I said.

"Thank you Master Daniel. I am telling you this in secret but tomorrow I am meeting in secret two ambassadors from our magical neighbours,"

"But your Father-" I started.

"My Father made a grave mistake when he foolishly ordered the assassination of the diplomats and Kings of our two most powerful neighbours,"

I couldn't deny that.

Taking a slip of the orange tea, my mouth exploded with wonderful sweet flavours of chocolate and lemon with a hint of sea salt. It was utter perfection.

"My Father thankfully failed to kill one of the Kings but I am hopeful that with me on the throne our relations can be improved. Thus the meeting tomorrow. Ordericous cannot afford it to fail. There are alliances being made against us. We must make our own,"

"And the Seeker?" I asked.

"He sent me a message. He has foreseen the location of the meeting. His forces will attack and if his Prophecy is to be believed this event will set us on the road to damnation,"

Me and mother looked wide eyed at each other.

"Where do we start?" we both asked.

"My agents inform me Lady Alessandria and her peer Nemesio is heading for a Waterfall thirteen miles northeast of here. Please travel there. You will find the information you seek,"

Mother got up, bowed and started to elegantly walk towards the doors.

"Thank you Lady Fireheart," the Queen said.

I too stood up and gave a mocking bow to my old friend before starting to walk away.

"Master Daniel, may I please have another moment of your time?"

I nodded and waved Mother to start walking to the horses without me.

When the doors shut, we both smiled at each other.

"She is still has scheming and elegant as always," the Queen said.

"You have no idea. I would ask and do a proper catch up but we both know I hate small talk. What's up?"

"I was discussing plans for a new armoured carriage with Master Gearing earlier and he made an odd comment,"

My stomach churned.

My dulled blade turned a little in my hand.

What did Harrison say?

"Master Gearing wanted to know if you were okay. He was concerned and he felt a little as if you were avoiding him. Then he rather shockingly went into details of your sex life. And I elegantly confirmed to him that it was not your sex life that caused you to avoid him,"

If the ground could swallow me up, I wish it did.

"Um I'm sorry?"

"Your sex life-"

"Yes your majesty I got that part. Is he really concerned? I'm not avoiding him. I love him more than anything,"

"Then please Master Daniel go and see him soon. I will send him a message telling him I have expressed my concern and you have confirmed your love. But I must ask you to complete my mission first. I love you and Harrison but my entire realm is at stake,"

I really wanted to say no to her and go to Harrison. I needed him and he needed me. Or at least he needed to know there was nothing wrong. I think. Something felt a little wrong.

But I had a mission to complete that would affect Harrison in the long run. I needed to protect the man I love.

With that, I simply bowed and went off to protect him in the long term. I just hoped when I returned our love was still there.

HEART OF PROPHENCY

CHAPTER 11

Looking back into the forest, Alessandria couldn't stop herself from focusing on every thick tree and twisted roots for the possible chance of the witches attacking them again. Not that Alessandria could do anything.

Sure she had some magic in her but that only allowed her to force people to tell the truth or see if they were lying. Not very useful skills of course if you're fighting powerful witches.

Feeling Nemesio's smooth fingers gently stroke her shoulder, she turned around to look at the impressive waterfall in front.

Alessandria smiled as she remembered jumping into the water as a child with her friends.

The waterfall must have been about twenty metres high with hundreds of litres of gushing water flowing every second.

The sound of it was immense. Alessandria could barely hear herself think.

It was beautiful though. As was the rocky circle around it with the pool of calm water at the bottom.

Hellen stepped close to the water and tasted some of it. She spat it out and shook her head.

Alessandria started to wonder what they were doing here. There was nothing. Nothing except droplets of water coating her skin and dampening her long hair.

At the least it was refreshingly warm.

The smell of sea salt made her puzzled but understand now why Hellen had spat the water out.

Feeling Nemesio standing next to her, Alessandria really wanted to lean into him and feel his heartbeat. But at the end of the day, she was their leader. And there was still something telling her loudly not to. Nemesio was the right man for her something told her. She just didn't know what.

Hellen gasped and shot back away from the water.

She grabbed her stick.

The water in the pool bubbled.

Alessandria grabbed her and stepped back.

She and Nemesio whipped out their swords.

The water bubbles immensely.

Something rose up.

A long scaly white neck covered in thick salt. It was like the white head of a dragon. Immense dagger like teeth shone in the sunlight.

Massive waves of water rushed off it.

The creature roared.

Revealing a massive salt-covered tongue.

Its large red eyes saw Hellen.

It charged at her.

Alessandria rushed over.

Swinging her sword into it.

Shards of salt smashed off.

The creature whipped its neck around.

Knocking Alessandria metres back.

The creature charged at her.

Nemesio stormed over.

The monster saw him. It screamed launching balls of salt at him.

Nemesio dived out the way.

Hellen whacked the monster with her stick.

Shards of salt shattered.

Hellen whacked it again.

A ball of salt shot out.

Hitting her in the stomach.

She collapsed to the ground.

She looked to be in agony.

Alessandria's eyes widened. Her rage built up.

Nemesio looked at her.

Alessandria nodded.

They both charged together.

The monster swung its mighty neck.

It hit Alessandria.

She landed with a thud on the ground.

Her hands hurting from the impact on the smooth wet rocks.

The neck slowed.

Allowing Nemesio to thrust his sword in its neck.

The monster screamed and screamed.

Alessandria jumped up.

Charging over to the creature.

It focused on her.

Allowing Hellen to whack its eye with her massive stick.

The monster screamed once again.

Salty grainy white blood poured from its eye.

Alessandria kept running.

She jumped into the air.

Aiming her sword.

The monster recovered.

It saw Alessandria.

The monster smiled.

Opening its mouth.

Alessandria's eyes widened as she saw roses upon roses of dagger like teeth.

They were getting closer.

Hellen's massive stick smacked into her.

Throwing her off course.

The monster dived for her.

Nemesio roared with fury as he ripped his sword out.

Thrusting it into the creature's eyes.

It screamed in utter agony.

Alessandria landed hard. Slicing her head on the rock and entire body flooding with pain from the flying stick.

She swore multiple times.

Why did Hellen have to throw her stick at her?

Alessandria thought she had shattered a rib or two.

Forcing herself over to her other side,

Alessandria saw the monster shriek a final time before it collapsed. Falling back into the pool of water.

The pool started to bubble furiously before the immense bones of the creature floated to the top. Licked clean of all its salty flesh.

Despite the air stinking of strange salt, Alessandria felt her body ease and almost felt healed.

Maybe this was some magical reward a warrior who was worthy of after defeating this beast?

Alessandria didn't care but she still bit her lip as she forced herself up.

Limping over to Nemesio and Hellen, she allowed Hellen to help her walk as they all looked at the immense bones in the pool.

"I really hope we didn't just kill what we were here for?" Alessandria said.

"Na, what could that beasty know about the Seeker?" Hellen asked.

Despite her having to take long deep breaths to control the pain, Alessandria nodded at Hellen's point. There had to be another reason.

"Nemmy? Oh Nemmy! What ya doing here?

CHAPTER 12

Now I've never minded the woods and forests of Ordericous but this forest is horrible. I mean Daniel Fireheart is known for lots of things, but I am not known for fighting my way through massive trees with twisted roots that seem to rise up whenever they get the chance.

This was ridiculous.

All around me are thick deadly trees that look like they could kill me with a breath. This is not my idea of a lovely day out with Mother.

And judging by the thick wet mud moving constantly under my feet as well as the look on Mother's face, she didn't disagree.

Taking a deep wet dew filled breathe, I turned my dulled blade between my fingers and focused on the very few positives that existed.

I even tried to focus on the water droplets covering my skin from the late afternoon… whatever happens in this forest.

Condensation- that's the word.

Attempting to ignoring the horrid damp air that stunk of decaying leaves and probably a dead fox.

I tried to look through the forest to see this waterfall we were heading to. No luck.

Hearing Mother swear repeatedly, I had to smile that I wasn't the only one not enjoying myself. I would easily stab someone about now.

Not Mother, of course.

Although, I have to admit Mother still looked great in her pitch black leather and metal armour. She looked like a perfect Knight. But I didn't feel safe around her.

A memory of me, Alessandria and dear Father came into my mind at the thought of going hiking in the mountains as children. It was beautiful but the mountains are dry, and they have snakes! Who doesn't love a good snake?

Stepping carefully over another massive root that looked more like a dead tree than a root, I allowed my mind to think about Harrison. My stomach churned at the thought of him being upset or even mad at me.

All I wanted was to be with him and love him. But he was right at least to some extent. I was avoiding him. I just don't know why. Maybe I should take up Alessandria's offer to talk and support me.

Granted I still have no idea what happened with her date with Nemesio. After what happened to me, a part of me wanted it to go badly but I do love my sister. And I do just want her to be happy. So I suppose I should hope it went alright.

"Daniel what do you think about the Queen's meeting?" Mother asked.

"It's a good idea. We all remember how futile her Father was,"

"Ha. He hated us, didn't he?"

"Only because of me," I said quietly.

Mother climbed over some more roots to catch up with me.

"Daniel, you know you aren't some burden right? You are my son and I love you,"

I nodded. There was something true in those words but sometimes I still feel like a burden. The entire reason why the other Houses and the Inquisition hated our House was because they were getting a gay protected.

And my favourite comment, I'm a risk to the integrity of the Ordericousian gene pool. I have to laugh at that. It's not like I'm going to have children and pass on my so-called gay genes. Even though there's no such thing.

"Do you think our neighbours will sign a treaty with the Queen?" I asked.

I whacked a fly away.

"I hope so Daniel. A trade treaty would prove fortunate for the House. More military assets for starters. Oh, hopefully I can convince the Queen to send troops over to our neighbours. Then they'll have to hire more troopers to reinforce Ordericous,"

"Do you just see this as a money-making opportunity?"

"Of course and if Alessandria is successful. You need to start thinking like this too."

I almost paused for a moment. The warmth and hope in those words were almost stunning. She really wanted us to be successful, but what was in it for her?

The air hummed violently with magical energy.

A fireball shot past.

A tree shattered.

Sending lethal wooden shards through the air.

I tackled Mother to the ground.

I jumped back up.

The three black cloaked witches were thirty metres behind us.

More fireballs roared through the air.

They exploded near mother.

The bestial, Flesheater part of me wanted to kill. Slaughter these women.

I wanted to eat their flesh and taste their blood.

I forced that part of me to stay in its bottle.

If I turned into a Flesheater.

I didn't know if I could return to being Daniel.

There was no Alessandria or Harrison here to help me.

More bright orange fireballs exploded.

I picked up Mother.

Throwing her over my shoulder.

We couldn't fight these witches.

We needed help.

I climbed rapidly over the roots.

My ankles wanting to turn and twist and break

on them.

I kept moving.

A fireball hit us.

The witches laughed.

Utter pain and heat flooded my body.

We fell forward.

Mother jumped off.

Another fireball hit her.

She screamed.

My Flesheater side stirred and twisted inside me.

I wanted, no needed to kill.

I needed to taste the flesh of mortals.

The sound of Mother crying in agony made me focus.

Rushing over to her, I saw some of the leather around her leg had been burnt off.

Revealing blistered and burnt skin.

The witches' laughter got closer.

We needed to move.

A thunderous roar ripped through the entire forest.

The witches stopped.

The air stopped humming with magical energy.

Another bestial roar ripped through the forest.

The witches flew towards us.

Something about them didn't make me want to attack them.

They flew straight past us.

They fled.

Helping Mother up, she cried a little as I helped her onwards. I hated to think about how painful it would be for her to walk another mile with these injuries.

"What was that noise?" I asked Mother.

"A demon,"

CHAPTER 13

The sound of footsteps splashing through puddles echoed around the dark cave as Alessandria, Hellen and Nemesio were led through the caves under the waterfall by Lady Serpentine.

Looking at the rough textured walls of the almost triangular cave, Alessandria couldn't believe she was walking with Lady Serpentine again. The head of the Criminal Underworld and an old lady who had a massive soft spot for Nemesio.

Alessandria couldn't entirely understand their odd relationship. She knew Nemesio had helped her to rise to the Head of the Underworld. But calling him Nemmy was just strange.

Breathing in the damp and probably mouldy air made Alessandria cough as they continued to walk further through the puddles of stagnate water.

The worse part though was the slight taste of dead decaying bird in her mouth. What Alessandria wouldn't give for some essential oils now to block out that smell.

Feeling the coldness of the water pulse through her leather boots and up her body reminded

Alessandria why she didn't come to visit. This was not her sort of place. And she was absolutely horrified when Hellen made a comment about coming here a few weeks ago to, quote on quote, sort out a brutish man at night. Did Hellen really have no boundaries when it came to her late night activities?

Looking straight ahead at the Lady Serpentine, Alessandria shook her head as she wouldn't believe this little old woman who looked as if she was about to die at any moment was controlling the entire underworld. With her shaky hands and dirty posh clothes. She admired the old lady. Alessandria hoped she could be this elegant and powerful at her age.

After a few more moments, the Lady led them into a massive cave opening tens of metres high and wide. Easily large enough to fit ten houses inside with massive puddles of freshwater inside. As well as a refreshing breeze of cool fresh air.

Lady Serpentine stopped and Alessandria walked over to see if she was okay.

"Oh Alessandria, I'm fine," Lady Serpentine said.

"I'm glad," Nemesio said, giving her a hug.

"It's just fabulous to see ya all again. Oh Nemmy, ya look great,"

Hellen tapped her massive stick on the ground.

Alessandria knew what she wanted or needed to ask.

"Lady Serpentine, we have-"

"Oh Alessandria, I know. Oh, I know. I see

all ya know. You and your brother being hunted by witches,"

"My brother!"

"Oh yes. He and ya Mother being hunted terrible. Now there's a local demon hunting outside. Oh, I hope they don't come across the demon,"

Alessandria's mind raced. She knew she had a mission to do but she had to protect her family.

"Listen here, Lady," Hellen said. "Tell us what we wanna know,"

"Oh Hellen. Is that an accent from the outskirts of Ordericous?"

Hellen nodded.

Alessandria wanted to hit herself.

"Oh Hellen that place. Some people say only scum live there. But there are some amazing criminals there. And those men-"

"As much as I love catch ups, we have a mission to do," Alessandria said.

Lady Serpentine nodded and looked at Nemesio.

"Please old friend. Help us," Nemesio said.

"Oh Nemmy, anything for you. What do ya need?"

"You said you see everything here. Please, where is the Seeker?" Alessandria asked.

The ground shook.

Chunks of rock fell from the ceiling.

"Oh dear. Oh dear. Those witches have come. Oh Nemmy, you and your friends must go,"

"Where?" he asked.

Alessandria looked around.

More chunks of rock smashed down.

"Oh Nemmy, there's a quarry. Three miles away. It's late now. Ya must not go tonight,"

Another violent shake.

Alessandria turned as she heard a rockfall in the distance.

Screams filled the caves.

Nemesio looked at Lady Serpentine. "It's time to stop hiding old friend,"

She nodded.

Alessandria cocked her head.

Lady Serpentine nodded.

Bright golden magical energy crackled around her.

"Go!" she boomed.

Alessandria's jaw dropped in amazement.

She was a witch!

Lady Serpentine whipped her hand rapidly in the air.

Some rock in the walls melted away. Revealing a staircase.

"Go!" she ordered.

Alessandria wanted to protest.

She couldn't let another person sacrifice herself.

Nemesio and Hellen started to run for the staircase.

Alessandria paused.

Lady Serpentine rushed over to her.

"Go! Live to fight another day. Remember the fate of the country rests on ya living. Take these," she said, forcing two circular symbols chunks of metal and a strange dagger into her hand.

It was her's and a Noble House's seal.

Two votes for her cause.

The three black cloaked witches appeared in the cave.

"GO!" she boomed.

Alessandria and her friends rushed away.

Hearing the staircase close behind them.

They kept running.

Guilt and failure filled Alessandria as she allowed another person to die for her mission.

No more.

That was not a promise.

That was truth.

CHAPTER 14

I know my autism means I am sort of limited in some emotions but Mother's crying is seriously annoying now.

No. Actually what's more annoying is I have no idea how to help her. I feel the need to help or comfort her but I just don't know how.

Thankfully, the thick dense forest with all those horrific roots were starting to give way.

A massive smile formed on my face as I realised we had left the forest and finally we had arrived at the waterfall. Or nearby.

In front of us was a massive beautiful river with rough white rapids and fast-flowing water. I made a note to myself not to fall in.

Then the smooth wet slippery grey rock on the banks of the river provided a very nice contrast for my booted feet as I carefully walked closer to the river.

The fresh smell of the life giving river made some tension leave me and my dulled blade slowed a little.

Placing Mother down carefully and I sat by her side with the river only a few metres away from her. I dipped my hand with a puddle of cold fresh water and splashed it over her burns.

Her eyes were still watery and she still bit her lip. I wanted to do more but I didn't know what to do. I supposed I should hug her but I really don't like physical contact. Carrying her for the last mile was a stretch for me.

Taking a few deep breaths, I tried to relax myself after all that contact. So my mind went to the place it felt safe- Harrison.

What I couldn't give just to see him and play with his longish beautiful hair. That would relax me. One of the few beautiful things that could manage to relax me. Just thinking about him made my body less tense. My dulled blade slowed.

The sound of the river plunging down further ahead made me sure we were close to the waterfall. But I and especially Mother needed to rest. We couldn't carry on.

A drop of Mother's blood made me closer to her. I was about brush it away and clear it with some more water but she grabbed my hand.

I tensed at the feeling of her smooth hand but I knew she was trying to be nice. So I made myself relax.

"Daniel, I know I haven't always been the most present of mothers. Especially since your father died-"

"But you were getting leverage to protect us," I said.

She rubbed her hand gently.

"Yes but I could have tried harder. I wish I could have been there when you were being abused and when you tried…"

She couldn't bring herself to say what I tried to do.

My arms burned at the reminder.

"What I'm trying to say is, if I don't make it today or whenever I do go. Just know I do love you and I want you to be happy. Be with Harrison. Change the law. Do whenever. Just. Be. Happy!"

She gently kissed my hand and rolled onto her side. Probably to take a nap and I couldn't blame her as I saw the sky starting to turn from deep orange to pitch blackness.

A part of me was surprised we had been in the forest for that long.

Then I fought about her words. Part of me thought this entire scheme wasn't about her getting anything. I think she wanted this to be about her family and most importantly she wanted to fix things between us.

A smile broke out on my face as I fought how we had both been abused by my brother Justin and… we had both been through so much. But she had finally said it- she wanted me to be with Harrison.

Maybe that was why I've been avoiding him. I didn't want him to suffer Mother's disproval for being a commoner. Sure that was part of it, but I still feel as if there was something more. Like another problem or concern I just couldn't place.

The ground below me moved.

Looking around, I couldn't see anything but I could have sworn I heard three sets of footsteps walking. And a massive wooden stick hitting stone.

Something moved under my bottom.

A large stick poked it.

I shot up.

"Daniel? What ya doing here?"

CHAPTER 15

Hearing the river roaring in front of her, Alessandria sat close to the edge staring into the forest on the other side. She could feel the presence of the night demon, or whatever it actually was, staring at her.

The large river roaring past her have Alessandria some comfort. The best case scenario would be the night demon tried to jump into the river and got washed away and fell off the top of the waterfall downstream. But she doubted that would happen quite so perfectly. And Alessandria doubted this so-called demon was stupid enough to try that.

Swirling her fingers over the smooth grey rock of the rover banks, Alessandria felt cold chills pulse up her arm. Then the fresh smell of smoke filled her senses, and oddly made her mouth taste like rabbit.

She admitted to herself that it was a surprise to see Daniel sitting on top of the staircase. It was great seeing them and knowing they were safe. But Alessandria frowned as she remembered the roar of that night demon and they decided to set up camp.

But that was all they could do. Just wait on the river banks til morning.

Turning around so she still sat down but faced the mini camp, Alessandria felt a moment of peace and calm for the first time all day.

She smiled as she saw her Mother and Hellen sleeping on a bunch of leaves and a pile of logs to raise them off the damp rock.

A part of her thought it was a shame that Mother said she had to go in the morning for a meeting with the Saga to discuss their progress.

Alessandria knew the real reason was so she would get in a few creature comforts, but maybe she would talk to her Mother. Maybe she could do something to the Saga for her as a favour?

Then Alessandria paused as she saw Nemesio there peacefully sleeping. Her Nemesio. Her strong beautiful man that had earned his place at her side. But why did she keep hesitating?

He did like her. He said that as much on their date and he had so many amazing stories. But- something was still making her resist him.

Telling herself to come back to that problem later, she moved her head and looked at the small but extremely warm fire that Daniel had built. The fire crackled and hummed as the twigs and small branches were devoured by the flames.

Then Alessandria noticed the only person who truly, truly cared for her sat on a large long log poking the fire. Her clever, beautiful brother.

Quietly wandering over to Daniel, she felt the warmth from the fire wash through her leather armour. Before she sat next to Daniel. Then she moved a few times to find a piece of log without a sharp knob sticking into her.

"She loves us you know, Mother," Daniel said.

Alessandria nodded.

"She... she even wants me to be with Harrison,"

Alessandria cocked her head in shock.

"I know. I was pretty shocked too," Daniel said.

Alessandria picked up a warm rough stick and poked the fire with it.

"Harrison came to see me today in the stables,"

Daniel smiled and shook his head.

"He went to see the Queen too but that time was more of an offhand comment,"

"I confirmed to him that you never stop talking about how wonderful he is. But I also know you have been avoiding him,"

Daniel stayed silent.

"Daniel I know we haven't been the closest until a few months ago but you are fairly passive aggressive towards the people you love. Yet I do know you well,"

He still stayed silent.

Alessandria smiled. "Daniel I'm your sister. Please, what's wrong?"

"I really do love him. Since I first saw him I've wanted to be with him,"

Alessandria blew on the fire. More flames erupted.

"But people always leave me,"

Alessandria looked at her brother not sure what to say.

"Whenever I get close to someone, something happens. Father died in the war. Harrison was forced away because of the lies. You-"

Alessandria placed a loving finger on his lips before lowering them.

"Daniel. Our lives are never easy. Especially yours. For that I am sorry. But life is about enjoying it. Making the most before something happens. You had hours each day with Father. I didn't. I had to do my military service and I went through my Nobility Princess phase,"

Daniel put a small log on the fire.

"Father loved you so much. Something can always happen. Don't let that define or rule you. Don't be scared of something that might not happen. Harrison loves you. You love Harrison. Just be with him,"

Alessandria placed her stick on the fire.

"And don't worry about the Church, the Inquisition, etc. I will deal with them. Just be with the man you love and talk to him. Tell him your concerns. He will understand,"

Daniel nodded. "Thank you,"

Alessandria smiled and leant back to pick up a largeish log behind her.

"And what about the man you love, Alessandria?"

Alessandria fell off the log. Landing on the smooth rock below before standing up and sitting back on the log.

"You never told me about your date,"

"Well-"

"Don't say it's private,"

"Fine. It was a great, amazing evening. We spent all evening and night exchanging stories. Our childhoods. Our dreams. Our past loves and missions. It was... so perfect,"

Daniel nodded.

"Nemesio was charming, handsome and so perfect. He was funny and everything I would ever want in a man,"

"But?" Daniel asked.

"But some of the stuff that haunts him troubles me. And how do I bring him into the Nobility? Isn't that unfair?"

Daniel cocked his head. "We all have baggage and things from our past. Me and Harrison both have the damage those lies did to us. I have the baggage of my arms and me trying to kill myself. None of this defines us or makes us worse partners,"

Alessandria slowly nodded. This is why she loved her brother. So practical. So annoyingly perfect in his answers. She knew he was right. Alessandria knew she was just making up an excuse.

"What about the Nobility?" Alessandria

asked.

"That I have no idea about. Me and Harrison we aren't *proper* Nobles. Harrison can't be in the Nobility unless he marries me. But Nemesio will be potential Nobility when your relationship becomes public,"

Alessandria placed her face in her hands.

"Meaning he will get all the media and other attention. But you must let him choose this or not? You cannot make this choice for him,"

Alessandria just looked at Daniel. "Since when did you become so wise?"

Daniel smiled and placed a final log on the fire.

Alessandria was about to hug him good night. But an immense roar ripped through the forest.

A loud scream echoed around.

Another roar came.

Trees collapsed in the distance.

It was all from this side of the river.

Alessandria grabbed her sword and Daniel and marched into the forest.

She had had enough of this Night Demon.

CHAPTER 16

I always knew Alessandria was the smartest person alive (well in terms of street smarts at least) but even I have to admit when she asked *good old Daniel* to help kill a demon. I really didn't expect to say yes.

Especially as I'm now surrounded by ugly thick dense trees with immense branches smashing into each other as the cool night breeze blows through the forest.

My limited exposed skin sent chills through me.

As I stood there pointlessly, I felt the soft mud starting to freeze and thankfully there were no more annoying roots.

My dulled blade spun slowly in my hand in an effort to stay warm, but I was failing. The night cold started to seep into me.

The smell of cold refreshing air made my lungs cold and my mouth taste of ice.

Having no idea where Alessandria was, I was really having my doubts about the plan. But if anything I (suppose) have absolute faith in my sister.

But my heart ordered my brain not to die. I couldn't die and not talk to Harrison one last time.

Deciding it was now or never, I started to shout to attract the beast and hopefully Alessandria would save me. Whilst I distract the creature.

And yes, it's an awful plan.

I continued shouting.

Then I stopped. It felt as if I was being watched.

I heard long claws slice into wood.

A tree fell.

Then another.

Then another.

Placing my hand on the freezing cold hilt of my sword, I slowly turned around to see the night demon.

I think demon is a perfect word.

The creature stood there. Its massive thick scaly black legs were twice the height of me. Its chest was cut and twisted deeply as if it was once something else.

Another tree fell.

Looking at the demon's arms they were massive. Muscular things covered in thick scales. But it's claws. They were as long as I was tall. And yet they had the power to destroy trees. But they looked as if they were implanted, not natural.

A loud hot breath shot out.

It smelt disgusting like rotting meat.

Against my better judgement, I looked at its face. I wanted to scream. It was awful. So unnatural.

There wasn't a face.

I could feel its warm, disgusting breath on me, but… it was impossible.

The demon roared.
I whipped out my sword.
The demon charged at me.
I dodged out the way.
Swinging my sword.
The demon dodged and laughed.
Trees collapsed all around me.
Lethal wooden shards charged at me.
I dived out the way.
Some shards hit me.
Digging into my flesh.
I could feel my warm beautiful blood drip down my arm.
I had to force the thoughts away.
My Flesheater ability couldn't come out now.
The demon charged.
It slammed into me.
Knocking me back.
I swung my sword.
It hit the creature's thick scales.
The sword did nothing.
The creature whacked my sword away.
My hand ached with pain.
My sword landed metres away.
I rushed over.
The demon sliced into my back.
More delicious blood ran from me.
No!
I could not lose control.
I spun around.

The demon was charging.

Alessandria dived from a treetop.

Landing on the demon's invisible head.

She drove her sword into its head.

Nothing happened.

The demon disappeared.

Alessandria fell.

The demon reappeared.

Raising its foot to stomp on Alessandria.

She rolled out the way.

I hated this.

The demon stomped.

It missed.

The demon thrusted its claws into the ground.

Alessandria was trapped between its claws.

The demon laughed in delight.

Her head was exposed.

Fear gripped me.

My beautiful blood ran down my back. I could feel my control weakening.

The demon raised its foot to stomp on her head.

I couldn't have that.

The bottle broke.

I stopped trying to control it.

My Flesheater ability flooded my system.

I screamed bloody murder.

My eyes turned glowing white.

My fingers and toes turned to lethal talons the size of swords.

My skin turned blood red and hardened.

The demon released Alessandria.

It looked at me.

My teeth turned to fangs.

I didn't care.

I needed to slaughter.

I needed to sink my fangs into warm fresh flesh.

The demon roared. Charging at me.

Alessandria screamed.

I surged forward.

Slashing the demon's chest.

It screamed in horror.

I could hurt it.

Warm beautiful blood covered my talons.

I swung again and again.

More blood and flesh was hacked off the demon.

It screamed and screamed in hope of salvation.

Utter delight filled me.

My fangs ripped into its flesh.

I chomped down on its demonic form.

Thick black smoke rose from the corpse as it died.

I didn't care. I just…

My eyes and everything returned back to normal.

I collapsed onto the floor. Gasping for air.

Alessandria rushed over and held me in her

arms. She hugged me so tight and rocked me gently.

I tried to wash the blood out of my mouth but there was something about the demon that puzzled me.

"What's wrong? You never return like that. Me or Harrison always has to convince you to turn back," Alessandria asked.

I looked over at the demon corpse to see nothing except the hacked-up body of a man.

"The demon. He wasn't a demon. He... was made. As I chomped on him, one of his memories played into my mind. A memory I wasn't meant to see. He served someone. Someone we know,"

"Who?"

"The Last Fateweaver," I said.

Alessandria dropped me.

I couldn't blame her. The Fateweavers- the most dangerous witch family in the world. A family of witches and warlocks capable of weaving the loom of fate into whatever outcome they wanted.

"You're wrong, Daniel. Father killed them all. He died stopping them," Alessandria said.

"He didn't," I said looking at the floor.

"What!"

"When I was in the Military. I made sure I investigated Father's death. The Last Fateweaver killed him or weaved the Fates to kill him. There is a final Fateweaver out there. A final person who could destroy everything we are trying to build!"

Alessandria collapsed against a tree.

I walked over to her and hugged her.

"We own it to Father and the entire world to find them and kill them,"

She nodded.

"I do know that Father's final action was chopping off his special organs. A witness told me before he was mysteriously killed a day later,"

"This is truly the Last Fateweaver,"

I nodded.

"Not a word to Mother. This stays between us. The Fateweavers were a plague to our family. I know Father did something to us to make sure we couldn't be influenced by them. We shouldn't worry her," Alessandria said.

I nodded.

Alessandria looked to the floor.

"What is it?" I asked.

"Lady Serpentine. She gave me a weapon but she said the fate of the entire world rests with my fate. She could have said life but she said fate,"

"Alessandria, one problem at a time but the entire world is in danger,"

CHAPTER 17

Feeling the rough sharp yellow stone beneath her feet, Alessandria stared down into the quarry below. Hundreds of metres of pure sharp lethal rock.

She had no interest in falling into the quarry.

It was so deep that she couldn't even see the bottom. Her best guess was a tiny blue mark all those metres below her. Maybe a lake?

The gentle early morning breeze blew through. It made a strange roaring sound of the wind whipping around the quarry. And coated her skin in a thin layer of sand and crushed up stone. The morning sun slowly rising behind her felt pleasantly warm against her skin.

She knew this was going to be a good day.

Placing her hand on the chilled hilt of her sword, she was really to use it and kill the Seeker.

Turning her head slightly to a small wooden ladder below, Alessandria knew it led to a cave entrance ten metres below them. Then they could slaughter the Seeker and stop him.

A small piece of doubt crept into her mind by now she knew to ignore it. There was always a chance of death but that was part of life. If she was going to die, Alessandria would die fighting.

Then she remembered the strange dagger Lady Serpentine had given her. It was so strange and weird. She had looked at it earlier. It was made from a glowing white crystal in the shape of a dagger. Alessandria could still feel its strange coldness in her fingers even now. She really hoped it worked.

Hearing a massive wooden stick scrape across the ground, Alessandria looked to see Hellen in her grey cloak ready for a fight. Followed by Daniel and the beautiful Nemesio close behind.

They were ready.

So she was.

The plan was simple. Climb down the ladder. Enter the cave. Kill the Seeker. Save the Queen. Simple.

Alessandria nodded.

They nodded back.

Alessandria climbed down the ladder. Its smooth wooden runners passing her fingers.

She landed on the ground.

The team followed.

The ledge was only a metre wide. Made from rough stone.

Alessandria saw the large cave entrance.

The team climbed down.

They all rushed over to the entrance.

They stopped.

A loud noise surrounded them.

Alessandria looked up.

Stone monkeys were climbed towards them.

They snapped their own bones. Throwing stony limbs at them.

The monkey's limbs grew back.

It was an ambush.

Alessandria ducked.

There was nowhere to go.

They were surrounded.

Hellen smashed them with her stick.

Daniel and Nemesio whipped out their swords.

Hacking them to pieces.

More monkeys kept coming.

Alessandria whipped out her sword.

Coldness covered her stomach.

She swung her sword.

Shattering a monkey.

The coldness grew in intensity.

She looked at her stomach.

Something bright white was glowing.

The dagger.

She whipped it out.

The crystal dagger burning her fingers.

The monkeys screamed.

Alessandria charged.

Thrusting the dagger into a monkey.

It turned to dust.

The monkeys paused.

Alessandria did not.

Her and her friends surged forward.

Slashing and lashing with their blades.

Alessandria sliced more monkeys.

They turned to dust.

They screamed.

The monkeys fled.

Alessandria looked at her team to make sure they were okay. Thankfully they were. The cold crystal dagger dimmed and Alessandria put it away. But she still had a job to do.

Everyone nodded.

They rushed over to the cave.

Their swords ready to kill.

The ground was smooth and wet.

Badly lit with only a few bring torches.

They kept walking.

Shadows moved constantly.

Sharp shards of rock rose up out of the ground.

Alessandria felt like she was being watched.

The monkeys turned up at the cave entrance.

They didn't come in.

They were guarding it.

Alessandria's stomach churned.

She hated this.

She knew the Seeker knew they were here.

They turned a corner.

The smell of bitter toxic smoke filled the air.

A burning torch pumped out black smoke.

Alessandria swung her sword.

Destroying the black smoke and torch.

Pitch blackness descended.

The stone monkeys laughed.
Alessandria could hear them moving.
Everyone kept running.
The ground turned uneven.
Alessandria lost her balance.
She fell.
The others ran past her.
Not knowing she had fallen.
She felt a stony hand touch her.
She screamed.
Swinging her sword.
Nothing.
More stony hands touched her.
She screamed.
A massive wooden stick and two swords swung. Shattering the monkeys.
Nemesio and Daniel grabbed her hand.
Hellen whacked more monkeys.
They charged down the cave.
They turned a corner.
A torch was burning.
Revealing a massive wooden door.
Alessandria could hear the monkeys.
They didn't know what was on the other side.
It could be a trap.
They didn't have a choice.
Alessandria broke the door lock.

CHAPTER 18

Alessandria kicked in the door.

I rushed in.

I heard my name and rushed over to help Nemesio lock the wooden door.

When the lock was thankfully in place, Nemesio sadly touched me. I quickly walked into the chamber whilst the others stayed by the door.

The sound of the stone monkeys banging and tapping on the wood door echoed all over the cave chamber. But the smell of freshly cooked rabbit was overwhelming as was the taste of juicy meat in my mouth.

As I walked further into the chamber, I spun my dulled blade quickly in one hand then I held the warm metal of my sword in the other.

But this chamber wasn't very impressive. You would have thought the so-called almighty Seeker would have a better lair.

This is rather stupid. There's a little ring of burning torches on the outside. Something made of straw resembling a bed and some ritualistic stone altar and- oh god. Tons and tons of sweet smelling tea leaves.

He was one of those people. A so-called tea leaf reader. A memory of tea leave reader from my childhood came into my mind. Saying I would marry the most beautiful woman ever. I have to laugh at her now. That clearly isn't going to happen. And I'm happy about that!

A loud bang came from the door.

The door started to crack.

Then it stopped.

The sound of little stone feet walking away filled our senses.

I crept forward.

Alessandria whipped out her sword towards me.

I spun around.

A large old man wearing long sweeping white silk robes appeared.

I whipped out my sword.

I charged.

A massive wooden staff appeared in his hand.

I swung.

He met my sword.

Magical energy crackled around us.

The others surged forward.

He dodged.

He jumped into the air swirling and twirling.

Hellen was thrown across the chamber.

I swung again.

He deflected the blow.

Alessandria roared.

She rapidly swung her sword.

As did Nemesio.

The Seeker was too busy.

I thrusted my blade into him.

He laughed.

My sword burnt red hot.

My hands burned.

Smoke poured from them.

I screamed.

Alessandria and Nemesio were thrown across the chamber.

They smashed into the rocky wall.

Someone grabbed me.

The cold metal of blade kissed my neck.

I could feel the Seeker's breathe in my ear.

"You not win, fool. I superior. I foreseen everything. I live. You die. It Prophecy," the Seeker said in a strange foreign accent.

"Mortisical?" I asked.

"No stupid boy. I from neighbouring country Eastern Aric. Strong people. Strong magic users,"

"But you lie, Seeker. There are no more magic users. You people were purged. I am sorry for that but you cannot come here and sow your seeds of trouble," Alessandria said.

He laughed. "The Heart of Fire right. My People were killed. I no Triad. I sow no seeds. I see seeds before grow,"

I struggled.

Hellen slowly walked around.

Nemesio walked the other way.

I struggled again.

"Stop moving!" he shouted.

I stopped for now.

Alessandria stepped forward. "What seeds of time have you seen? What is the Triad planning?"

"Three came me. They wanted know things. I told what they need. They one who killed. I tried warn him. He stupid,"

Alessandria rolled her eyes.

"You asked Triad is doing. Wrong question. I have seen something. You not kill me. My witches rogue. They attack meeting. I told them,"

I smiled. We had what we needed. This Seeker wasn't going to tell us anything.

The metal slashed across my throat.

I screamed.

He released me.

Alessandria rushed forward.

My hands clunked my throat.

Thick rich red blood covered them.

My Flesheater ability screamed inside me.

It didn't know what to do.

It needed me to survive.

I couldn't activate it.

Alessandria grabbed me.

"It is Prophecy,"

"Bastard!" Alessandria shouted.

She charged forward.

Nemesio and Hellen joined her.

More blood flooded out of my neck.

I tried to activate my Flesheater ability.

It wasn't working.

The skin around my neck hardened.

That was it.

The blood slowed a little.

Alessandria slashed and lashed and swirled her sword at the Seeker.

She sliced him.

He threw them all across the room.

The Seeker disappeared.

He reappeared over me.

He grabbed my throat.

More blood came out.

My mind aching.

My feet were numb.

Alessandria tackled him.

Throwing me to the ground.

My head smashed into some rock.

Slicing my head.

Alessandria's stomach glowed bright white.

It was almost blinding.

The Seeker whacked her.

Hellen whacked him in the head.

Black blood sprayed up the walls.

Nemesio swung his sword.

The Seeker blocked it.

Lightning shot out of his hand.

Hitting Nemesio.

Nemesio fell to the ground shaking.

Smoke poured from Alessandria's stomach.

She whipped out the glowing white crystal dagger.

The Seeker disappeared.

A wooden staff whacked me around the face.

My legs went completely numb.

My body flooded with pain.

Two hands picked me up by the throat.

More dark rich blood flooded out. Covering the Seeker's hands.

I looked at Alessandria.

The Seeker dug his long nails into my throat.

Opening up the wound.

Alessandria threw me the crystal dagger.

I caught it.

Thrusting it into his arm.

The arm turned to crystal.

Hellen whacked it.

Shattering it.

He dropped me.

I grabbed him by the head.

"Prophecies can be rewritten," I said, thrusting the dagger into his chest.

I collapsed.

His body turned to crystal.

As his body turned, he looked at Alessandria.

"The Sword is your boss," he said.

Hellen whack shattered him.

My vision turned to blackness and I couldn't

feel my body anymore.

I thought I could hear Alessandria saying something but it sounded miles away.

My mind filled with memories of Harrison. I hated that I was going to leave him like this.

Pain shot up my arm.

My hand holding the crystal dagger burned me.

It felt like lava was being poured onto my hand.

I felt something moving up my arm into my body and mind.

A memory of the Seeker played inside my head.

He was explaining the secret meeting to the three black cloaked witches.

Then the memory died.

His life energy filled me.

My eyes opened.

I shot up.

Gasping for air.

I looked down at the dagger. It was gone but I rolled up my leather sleeves and all my old deep cuts were glowing bright white as something continued to move up into my body.

Looking over to where the Seeker's crystal shards should be, I only saw cold lifeless stone.

For some reason the dagger had saved me. I didn't know why but I was going to make the most of this new life.

HEART OF PROPHENCY

I jumped up.
Running for the door.
Remembering there was a Queen to save.

CHAPTER 19

With the wind whipping through her long hair, Alessandria rode on.

The hooves of horses pounding into the hard sun baked ground as they rode.

Nemesio, Hellen and Daniel rode close behind her. They had to save the Queen.

The smell and taste of foul smoke and burning wood confirmed Alessandria's worst fears as they rode.

As the horse pounded along, Alessandria could barely see the thick trees on either side of the large hard dirt road.

She looked ahead. Seeing a massive round hut the size of a football pitch. Immense flames consumed the thatch roof.

The white paint melted off. The roaring flames filled the air.

They had to hurry.

Alessandria dug her heels into the horse making it go faster. As she thought about the horror of finding the Queen's body. She sadly doubted the same trick would bring back Daniel.

As Daniel's horse caught up, Alessandria smiled. She was more than glad the trick had worked. Even though, he was covered in his own blood and had a whacking great scar across his throat.

She whipped her head round to see Nemesio. Alessandria had to make sure he was okay. She needed him.

The smell of smoke grew in intensity.

The air hummed with magical energy.

Roars of flames grew louder.

They arrived outside the massive hut.

The heat from the fire made Alessandria sweat.

They needed to move.

She waved them along.

Alessandria jumped off her horse.

The sun-baked ground feeling too solid as she landed.

Everyone ran over to the small wooden doorway.

The door was gone.

Turned to ash.

A scream came from inside.

They charged in.

Alessandria and others entered a massive circular bare chamber.

Wooden beams fell from the roof.

Flames erupted.

Alessandria jumped out the way.

Sweat poured down her.

Smoke covered her vision.

Alessandria couldn't see anyone.

She felt alone.

She heard a shout in an ancient language.

Half of the hut exploded outwards.

The smoke rushed away.

Her vision cleared.

Alessandria coughed.

She looked up.

The Queen stood there in a stunning white dress.

Swirling and twirling her two long golden glowing swords at the enemy.

The three black cloaked witches launched a volley of fireballs.

The Queen dodged them.

Alessandria couldn't see the Ambassadors.

The Queen hissed in pain.

Her Queen needed her.

Alessandria rushed over.

The others followed.

Alessandria screamed in rage at the foes.

The witches turned.

Air crackling with utter power.

Two witches zoomed over.

One tackled Alessandria.

The other witch got whacked by Hellen.

Hellen whacked the witch again and again.

Nemesio and Daniel rushed over to protect the Queen.

Alessandria was thrown to the ground.

Her head tapping the hard ground.

The witch punched her.

Alessandria slapped her.

The witch headbutted Alessandria.

The witch smashed her fists into Alessandria's chest.

She got winded.

Alessandria could feel the witch smile.

Hellen whacked the witch off her.

Alessandria jumped her.

They looked at the smashed-up body of the other witch.

Hellen smiled at her massive stick.

The witch that attacked Alessandria screamed at Hellen.

All three women charged.

The Witch launched torrents of black flames at them.

Alessandria pushed Hellen out the way.

The fire touched Alessandria.

She screamed.

Daniel tackled the witch.

His teeth growing longer.

Alessandria needed to stop this.

If the ambassadors were alive Flesheaters couldn't be common knowledge.

The witch screamed.

Launching fireball after fireball.

It was useless.

Alessandria rushed over.

Thrusting her sword into the witch's chest.
Black blood sprayed out.
She grabbed Daniel.
Hugging him tight.
He pushed her carefully away.
Alessandria looked at him.
His teeth were normal.
The Queen roared behind him.
They spun around.
The Queen swirled her glowing swords at the witch.
The Witch threw the Queen across the room.
Her glowing swords flew out of her hands.
Alessandria and Daniel rushed over.
Nemesio jumped into the air.
The Witch saw him.
Nemesio screamed.
His eyes bulged.
Blood ran out of his nose.
Alessandria couldn't lose him.
She grabbed a boiling hot piece of ceiling.
She couldn't care it was burning her.
She launched it at the witch.
It hit her.
The witch's black cloak caught.
Flames engulfed the witch.
Nemesio fell to the ground.
Daniel and Alessandria kept charging.
They both readied their swords.
The Witch screamed.

The air crackled with magical lightning.

It wasn't controlled.

It was chaos.

Alessandria and Daniel charged over to the witch.

Raised their swords.

And bought them down.

Both swords slaughtered the witch.

Thick oily black blood sprayed up the walls.

Another wooden beam collapsed.

Thick black smoke filled the air.

Daniel rushed over to the Queen. Picking her up and her swords.

Hellen found the two ambassadors and helped them out.

Alessandria didn't care.

She needed Nemesio.

She rapidly looked around.

Nemesio was lying metres from her.

Alessandria rushed over.

Daniel shouted at her from the doorway.

A massive wooden beam collapsed.

Blocking the door.

Alessandria picked up Nemesio.

Throwing him over her shoulder.

She looked around for an exit.

There wasn't one.

She didn't want to die.

She needed to tell Nemesio she loved him.

Thick white smoke came from flames twenty

metres away.

Alessandria didn't know why but she ran.

The flames cleared.

Alessandria jumped through the white smoke.

She landed on the hard rough ground.

Dropping Nemesio.

Daniel quickly picked up the Queen's swords and his leather trench coat.

She didn't know what happened.

She didn't care.

Alessandria rushed over to Nemesio.

Stroking his face.

Willing him to wake up.

He didn't.

The Queen elegantly wrapped her old friend in her arms. Alessandria forced her face into her dress.

"What's wrong?" Nemesio asked, coughing.

Alessandria pushed the Queen away and hugged Nemesio. The man she loved was alive and most importantly it was over. It was all over.

CHAPTER 20

Despite me knowing I was covered in my own dark rich red blood, I had to see Harrison. As soon as we had all escorted the Queen and the ambassadors back to the castle. I left and just badly needed to see him.

As I quickly walked down the long corridor down to the engineering department, I still shook my head at these smooth grey stone walls that lacked personality, and I felt the rough chipped stone floor under my feet.

Ahead I saw the large wooden and Iron doors to the engineering department as well as I smelt the typical oil that my beautiful Harrison came home smelling like every night. I could almost taste his lips now.

I missed him.

But most of all I was nervous. I was really, really nervous about seeing Harrison. What if he was mad at me? What if he wanted to break up? What if-

I stopped myself and focused on what I could control. I loved him more than anything else in the world.

I loved how he made me laugh and how he comforted me. How he never judged me and how he never mocked me. Like so many others.

Seeing I was just a few steps away from the door, I stopped.

My palms hot and sweaty at the thought of seeing him. One of my earliest memories of him played in my mind a simple meaningless memory to him but a meaningful one to me. I wasn't friends with him at the time but three boys were bullying me because of my autism. They broke my arm. Then no reason at all Harrison helped me. He stood up to them. Sent them to the hospital. He got expelled for a week but he didn't care. He helped me when no one else ever did.

That is what the man I love is like.

My palms were really hot now.

Taking a deep breath, I slowly turned the warm doorknob and stepped inside.

Shutting the door loudly behind me, I was impressed how they redecorated after what happened with the Triad assassins. All the rows upon rows of beautiful black and red wooden carriages went on for miles down my right hand side.

Then to my left was a very impressive workshop filled with tens of large silver cabinets filled with tools I have no idea what they're for.

Breathing in the oily air, I looked for my beautiful man. He was nowhere to be seen. I knew it was late in the afternoon so all the engineers should be gone but Harrison was committed to his work (and me) so he was still here.

I knew it.

"Danny?"

I turned around to see my beautiful Harrison come out from the rows of carriages. He gave me a smile which quickly turned to worry when he saw the blood all over my throat.

I didn't care.

I rushed over to him. Wrapping my arms around his amazing slightly muscular body. And giving him a massive hug. Resting my face into his stunning longish blond hair.

"What happened to you?" Harrison asked.

I didn't need to worry him or explain myself to him just yet. I placed my lips onto his. His lips tasting as fresh and beautiful as always.

I broke away after a few seconds. "I'm sorry. I am so damn sorry,"

Harrison continued to hold me tight.

"Did Alessandria tell you?" he asked.

"And the Queen?"

He gently hit his head on my shoulder.

"She was very diplomatic. I think she found it funny," I said.

"I am right?"

"Maybe. I love you so much Harrison but you are right. I guess I have been avoiding you,"

He raised his head and rested his forehead against mine.

"I'm scared. We're great. Things have never been better. This is when things usually happen. My Father died. My Sisters leave me. The lies that broke us apart. All happened when things were at the height of those relationships. I don't want to lose you. It's not fair on you,"

Harrison smiled. "Stop being scared. I would rather lose you to a real threat than a made up one. Things are different anyway. We both have friends in high places,"

I nodded.

Harrison cupped my face in his hands and kissed my forehead.

My eyes widened. That was a little strange.

"I want to prove my love to you," he said.

I cocked my head.

Harrison got down on one knee.

"Daniel Fireheart, will you marry me?"

CHAPTER 21

Returning to where it all began only yesterday morning, Alessandria felt the smooth freshly polished marble floor under her feet as she walked. And she breathed in the surprisingly pleasant chemicals that filled the art gallery. Was that a hint of lemon and lime? Even if they weren't the taste still lingered on her tongue.

Then Alessandria stopped in front of the beautiful painting from yesterday of the impressive naval battle with its amazing brushstrokes of the waves, ships and even the little detailed faces of the soldiers waiting for the ground assault.

However, unlike yesterday, Alessandria now knew what her favourite piece of the painting was. It had to be the little detailed troopers. Not only for the truly amazing artistry that went into painting so many faces on such a large canvas. But for the fact that these people weren't the obvious heroes, like her.

For the Queen had agents, soldiers, a navy and so many other noisy people who would happily take the credit and not save the day. But her and her friends did save it. They didn't want any special treatment or rewards. They were doing their jobs and that's what Alessandria lived for. She lived to serve her Queen and protect her no matter the cost.

Noticing the warmish sunlight from the little window behind her coating her skin, Alessandria noticed that it was a lot nicer were in the evening after closing time. At least there were no sweaty people around. Maybe she would book after hours more often.

Then her mind drifted to the amazing news that Daniel and Harrison were getting married. Even the thought of getting a brides- Groomsmen(?) dress got her excited. She was finally going to attend a wedding and a real wedding. Not the normal fake wedding in the nobility. But two people that loved each other. That is what made it perfect for Alessandria.

But would she have to teach Hellen how to behave?

Oh god, what if Hellen bought her massive stick in? What would she do whack a waiter to get another drink?

Alessandria made a mental note to meet up with Hellen tomorrow. Then she cocked her head. When was the wedding?

That was a problem for another time.

The sound of Nemesio's footsteps made Alessandria smile a little and she looked briefly in his direction. Admiring his beautiful face and eyes and how he moved so confidently in his red and black armour.

Her smile deepened when she smelt his earthy aftershave and noticed a red letter in his hand.

She knew exactly what that was.

"Beautiful, isn't it?" Alessandria asked, pointing to the painting.

"It is. Both of you are,"

Alessandria smiled deepened once more. "What's that in your hand?"

"A signed letter from the Queen confirming the Saga of the Blessed Earth is dead. Natural causes they said,"

Alessandria couldn't stop smiling.

"We both know it wasn't natural in the slightest,"

Alessandria stopped smiling. "If this was murder then I would have to congratulate the killer. The Saga was horrible and at least Daniel can be safe now,"

She wanted to go on and said that the Saga deserved it and she would do anything to protect Daniel. But Alessandria wanted to give Nemesio a piece of deniability in case someone found out.

Nemesio passed her another letter.

Alessandria beamed. "Very Nice. The Saga signed off on her pledge to our cause before she sadly died. Now no one will recant it. No one would dare go against the wishes of a dead Saga,"

"Keep reading,"

"Even better, the Order of the Precious Metal has pledged to,"

At last, Alessandria was finally on the home stretch of her mission. She had to get the law changed. She couldn't be the Head of her Noble

House.

"How many left?" Nemesio asked.

"The House of the Blueheart, the Church and the last two Inquisitorial Orders,"

Nemesio almost laughed. "The Church will not agree to your law change. And it's great news about Daniel,"

Alessandria ignored him. He had a point but she was more concerned about the wedding. Sure, gay marriage was legal in Ordericous but it wasn't done before. Probably because the church had to sanctify all marriages. Yet another problem for tomorrow.

"I will make them pledge. I will make them all pledge," Alessandria said.

Nemesio stepped closer. "I know. I will always help you,"

Alessandria turned to face him. She breathed in his earthly aftershave. But before she could speak Nemesio said something.

"What did the Seeker mean by the Sword is your boss? Do you have a boss?"

Alessandria paused for a minute.

"No. I am a Dominicus Procurator. There is no one above me in my land,"

"In other lands?"

"Each land of this country is controlled by the Queen or a Noble House. We all answer to the Queen. No one else can overrule us,"

"Well, it's not the Queen," Nemesio said.

Alessandria just looked at him.

Nemesio stepped closer and placed his arms carefully around her.

"I won't bit you," she said.

"I don't know. I felt sorry for that steak on our date. We'll deal with the Flamesword tomorrow,"

Alessandria hugged him.

"Where does this lead us, Lady Alessandria? I know you've been distant since our date. Did I do something wrong?"

And there was the question.

Alessandria still held him.

"I know I have and I'm sorry. Our date was great. I loved it. It's just…"

"What?"

"I spoke with Daniel and I said I'm worried about you. If we get together even before we're married, if that happens, the media and people will be interested in you. They will want to know EVERYTHING about you. Even your time in the Inquisition,"

Nemesio frowned.

"I do have feelings for you Nemesio. I just don't want you to get involved in something that you didn't know about,"

He gave her a massive smile. "You have feelings for me?"

Alessandria nodded.

"It is still early, my Lady. We could get some dinner. There's a nice restaurant a few blocks away,"

Alessandria looked at the painting. "Sorry.

Can't. Grab that edge of the painting,"

    Alessandria grabbed one side of the painting.

    Nemesio grabbed the other.

    "Why?"

    "Because I want this in my room. We're *borrowing* it,"

Author's Note

Thank you for reading that I really hope you enjoyed it.

For me this was a great book to write. I had so much fun with it because there were so many things I wanted to explore.

For example, I always knew by the end of this story that Daniel and Harrison were going to get engaged. But I didn't know how or what was going to make them get engaged.

Hence, why I littered the story was small doubts about their relationship and what was going on.

Personally, I'm really excited about the challenges they might face.

Another thing I wanted to explore what the relationship been Daniel and his Mother because let's face it. We all know Kinaaz is a scheming and very clever woman, but why?

So that's why I made sure Daniel and his Mother had some of the conversations they did. As well as I needed to explore what their relationship was because in book one we know that Justin abused both of them.

That was interesting to explore.

Then the final main feature of the book I needed to explore was: what happened between Alessandria and Nemesio on their date?

Part of me wanted to do this as a little short story but then you get into the stories issues because something dramatic or interesting would have to have happened. And I wanted the data to go perfectly.

So Alessandria couldn't say "The date was awful I don't want to be with him,"

However, my favourite part of the book, in addition to when Harrison proposes to Daniel, is the last chapter. Because Alessandria confesses to us, the readers, that she killed the Saga.

That was definitely a WHAT! moment for me. Because we all imagine Alessandria has a good person who always acts legally and wants to protect her family and Queen. So for her to break the law and murder this Saga is impressive, and it just goes to show how far she is willing to go to protect her family. But most of all Daniel.

Overall, I really hoped you enjoyed the book as much as I did.

Please see the FREE and EXCLUSIVE short story on the next page and Alessandria and the gang will see you in *Heart of Bones!*

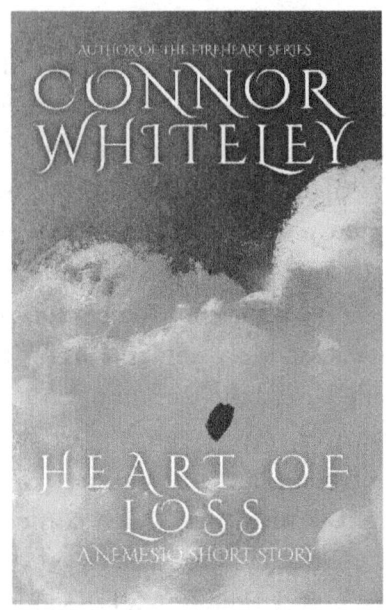

GET YOUR FREE AND EXCLUSIVE SHORT STORY NOW! LEARN ABOUT NEMESIO'S PAST!

https://www.subscribepage.com/fireheart

Thank you for reading.

I hoped you enjoyed it.

If you want a FREE book and keep up to date about new books and projects. Then please sign up for my newsletter at www.connorwhiteley.net/

Have a great day.

About the author:

Connor Whiteley is the author of over 30 books in the sci-fi fantasy, nonfiction psychology and books for writer's genre and he is a Human Branding Speaker and Consultant.

He is a passionate Warhammer 40,000 reader, psychology student and author.

Who narrates his own audiobooks and he hosts The Psychology World Podcast.

All whilst studying Psychology at the University of Kent, England.

Also, he was a former Explorer Scout where he gave a speech to the Maltese President in August 2018 and he attended Prince Charles' 70th Birthday Party at Buckingham Palace in May 2018.

Plus, he is a self-confessed coffee lover!

HEART OF PROPHENCY

OTHER SHORT STORIES BY CONNOR WHITELEY

Blade of The Emperor

Arbiter's Truth

The Bloodied Rose

Asmodia's Wrath

Heart of A Killer

Emissary of Blood

Computation of Battle

Old One's Wrath

Puppets and Masters

Ship of Plague

Interrogation

CONNOR WHITELEY

Other books by Connor Whiteley:

The Fireheart Fantasy Series

Heart of Fire

Heart of Lies

More Coming Soon!

The Garro Series- Fantasy/Sci-fi

GARRO: GALAXY'S END

GARRO: RISE OF THE ORDER

GARRO: END TIMES

GARRO: SHORT STORIES

GARRO: COLLECTION

GARRO: HERESY

GARRO: FAITHLESS

GARRO: DESTROYER OF WORLDS

GARRO: COLLECTIONS BOOK 4-6

GARRO: MISTRESS OF BLOOD

GARRO: BEACON OF HOPE

GARRO: END OF DAYS

Winter Series- Fantasy Trilogy Books

WINTER'S COMING

WINTER'S HUNT

WINTER'S REVENGE

WINTER'S DISSENSION

Miscellaneous:

THE ANGEL OF RETURN

THE ANGEL OF FREEDOM

CONNOR WHITELEY

All books in 'An Introductory Series':

BIOLOGICAL PSYCHOLOGY 3RD EDITION

COGNITIVE PSYCHOLOGY THIRD EDITION

SOCIAL PSYCHOLOGY- 3RD EDITION

ABNORMAL PSYCHOLOGY 3RD EDITION

PSYCHOLOGY OF RELATIONSHIPS- 3RD EDITION

DEVELOPMENTAL PSYCHOLOGY 3RD EDITION

HEALTH PSYCHOLOGY

RESEARCH IN PSYCHOLOGY

A GUIDE TO MENTAL HEALTH AND TREATMENT AROUND THE WORLD- A GLOBAL LOOK AT DEPRESSION

FORENSIC PSYCHOLOGY

THE FORENSIC PSYCHOLOGY OF THEFT, BURGLARY AND OTHER

HEART OF PROPHENCY

CRIMES AGAINST PROPERTY

CRIMINAL PROFILING: A FORENSIC PSYCHOLOGY GUIDE TO FBI PROFILING AND GEOGRAPHICAL AND STATISTICAL PROFILING.

CLINICAL PSYCHOLOGY

FORMULATION IN PSYCHOTHERAPY

PERSONALITY PSYCHOLOGY AND INDIVIDUAL DIFFERENCES

CLINICAL PSYCHOLOGY REFLECTIONS VOLUME 1

CLINICAL PSYCHOLOGY REFLECTIONS VOLUME 2

Made in the USA
Monee, IL
03 May 2026

49438375R00085